CAUGHT!

Keane rolled out. A bullet smashed the rocks just in front of him and he froze as an older man stepped around the shoulder of sandstone with a rifle in his hands. Keane set the revolver down and raised his hands.

"Surrendering will not save you, *señor.* Nothing will now," the Mexican said with a cool certainty. He shouted up the hill. "Santiago! I have the man."

After a moment a face appeared from behind another rock up the slope. "Shoot the bastard," the man ordered. "Shoot him now, then we will finish off the other one, like we should have last night!"

Suddenly a rock whizzed through the air and smacked solidly into the Mexican's jaw. It knocked his head sideways and his finger involuntarily squeezed the trigger. The bullet flew wide. Keane grabbed up his revolver and fired.

THE OUTCASTS

THE OUTCAST BRIGADE

JASON ELDER

LEISURE BOOKS NEW YORK CITY

A LEISURE BOOK®

March 2000

Published by

Dorchester Publishing Co., Inc.
276 Fifth Avenue
New York, NY 10001

ISBN 0-8439-4699-7

THE OUTCAST BRIGADE

Chapter One

"That's all there is too it, Nantaje. The matter is closed."

"If you do this, the army . . . it leaves me with nothing."

Captain McGowan's gray eyes narrowed at the young Apache scout standing before his desk. "Did you have anything when you came in?" he snapped.

"But General Crook—"

"General Crook is no longer in charge here. General Miles is, and the policy has changed." McGowan's voice moderated a bit. "I'm sorry, Nantaje, but that's how it is. Neither Miles nor Sheridan ever agreed with Crook's policy of using Apache scouts, and now that he has been transferred, Miles is letting them all go. Besides, the Apache problem is pretty much in hand. Geronimo will be taken soon, and the other chiefs are already on the reservation or on their way to Florida. There just isn't any need for your kind anymore."

Nantaje's long black hair glistened in the sunlight flooding through the window. "You are wrong, Captain McGowan."

7

His dark eyes fixed upon the officer's face. "I did have something before I came here."

McGowan reached for a pen and signed his name to the bottom of a piece of paper. "And what might that be?"

"My nation."

The officer looked up, frowning, then handed the paper across to him. "This is your discharge. Take it to the paymaster. He will square you up to today. I want you off the post by nightfall. Understand?"

"I understand. I understand more than you think." Nantaje started for the door.

"Oh, and one other thing."

He looked back.

"Turn your rifle in at the armory. You can keep the horse." McGowan grinned. "See, you are leaving with more than you came with."

Outside, Nantaje paused before the sharp slash of sunlight beyond the porch and squinted past the glaring tin roofs at the hazy hills to the west. His gaze lowered and moved across the adobe and frame buildings. A hot wind snaked through the outpost, shaping a small funnel out on the baked clay on the parade ground. The wind momentarily stirred the Stars and Bars hanging limp from the tall, white flagpole, then passed, leaving Fort Bowie simmering under a scorching summer sun.

But the Apache didn't notice the heat as he stepped out of the shade beneath the porch roof of the adjutant's office and started across the parade ground.

"Nantaje."

To his right a man waved from the open door of one of the officers' quarters. Hitching a suspender strap over his arm, Lt. Bud Wilson left the shade of the doorway and came bareheaded across the parade ground. "How did it go with McGowan?" he asked, shading his eyes and falling in step with the Apache.

Nantaje managed a small smile for his old friend. He

and Wilson had ridden together a lot of years . . . but that had been back when General Crook was in command. Since Miles had taken over, Nantaje had seen little of Wilson.

"Captain says they don't need Apaches to scout for the army."

"It's this new command, I'm afraid. Times are changing. What's that?"

Nantaje waved the paper in the hot air. "I think it is what you white men call 'walking papers.' "

"That's too bad. They use you up then toss you away," Wilson lamented philosophically. "Well, you aren't the only one, you know. We've lost a lot of good men recently, white and Apache. I'm going to miss you." Wilson grabbed Nantaje's right arm. "The team is going to miss you out there on the mound. You've got one hell of a fast-ball, Nantaje."

The Apache grinned. "If you can keep Corporal Miller from guard duty so much, you wouldn't need my right arm." He gave a short laugh. "At least McGowan let me keep the horse."

"Big deal. What are you going to do now?"

He stopped, his dark face revealing no emotion. "Don't know. Maybe I will go find what is left of my people."

"You know where they are?"

The tight line of his lips lifted into a thin, knowing smile. "I did not tell the army everything."

"You sly dog."

Nantaje laughed and they resumed their march across the parade ground.

"I'll miss you. You're the best damned tracker I've ever known, Nantaje. If you ever need references, just send them by to see me." Wilson smiled, remembering. "We had us some good times, didn't we?"

"Yes. Some good times. Some not so good. I will miss you, too, Wilson."

At the paymaster's door, Wilson clasped the Apache's hand one last time and pumped it mightily. "You take care of yourself, Nantaje. Maybe someday our paths will cross again. Till then, all my best."

The late-afternoon Arizona sun glinted dull red off the lenses of Sgt. Sam Butler's field glasses as they followed the rider below. A tight grin creased Butler's face and he passed the glasses to Corp. Conrad Gunther, sprawled on the hot rocky ground beside him. "There's our boy."

Butler glanced back at the six men tucked out of sight behind the rugged bluffs where ocotillo, stiff desert grasses, sage, and creosote clung to the rocky soil. The men took what shade they could find among the rocks while their horses grazed in a swale splashed bright green from the paloverde growing there. What a desolate land, Butler thought. He could never figure out what all the fuss was about. If it was up to him, he'd happily leave it all to the scorpions, rattlesnakes, and Apaches.

"It's him, all right," Gunther confirmed.

Butler scooted down the back side of the rise. "He's coming."

"The Apache?" Walt Green asked, scratching the stubbly growth on his chin.

"Who else do you think he means, bullet head?" a man in frayed blue trousers scoffed from the shade of a tall rock.

Green wheeled toward Peter Hennigan, but before he could retaliate, Conrad Gunther came scrambling down off the slope, sending a cloud of dust and stones clattering before him. "He's heading south, just like you reckoned he would, Sam."

"We're in luck, boys. If that 'pache is going where I think he is, we'll have us another fine shipment for Ortega and friends. Get off of your asses and get ready to mount up." Butler turned toward the graying man with faded sergeant's stripes on the sleeve of his blue uniform blouse. "Think you can keep that 'pache in sight till we see for sure where he's going?"

Jon Setter spat a stream of tobacco juice at a lizard sunning on the side of a rock. He missed and the reptile darted into a dark crevice. "Been following the Apaches for nearly ten years, Sam. Can't see as this one will be any different."

"Get to it, then. Make damned sure you don't lose him. We'll be behind you a ways so that Injun don't get suspicious."

Setter swung up onto his horse and started off on the Apache's trail while the others gathered their gear and mounted up. At Butler's orders, they moved out, following Setter and the Indian.

The trail cut south along the eastern lift of the Chiricahua Mountains. Nantaje followed it until late in the day; then he suddenly turned his horse to the west and into the mountains, where he made camp at Ham Springs. Early the next morning he pushed on toward Camp Rucker, but he swung wide of the small army outpost by a couple of miles and crossed the pass to the south, working his way up over the ridge and then down into Horseshoe Canyon.

On the canyon floor a trickle of water ran away to the east. Nantaje reined to a halt and watered the animal. He thrust his head in the cold water and drank deeply of it himself, then rested in the shade of a gnarled cedar. His dark eyes scanned the rugged landscape, searching, probing the shadows and clefts. He'd not been at ease since leaving the fort, and he wondered if it wasn't just the cool welcome he knew he'd get upon returning to his people.

Although the White Mountain Apaches had never taken part in the wars with the white man, he had many friends, many family members who had. Some would even consider him a traitor for his work with the army, and he didn't think he would be warmly welcomed back into the camp.

But he had a sister and nephew there, and a brother-in-law whom he wanted to see again.

Nantaje climbed back onto the horse, the uneasiness still with him and growing. Instinctively he cast a glance down his back trail. A flash of light in the distance caught his eye, but it was only a raven winging into view, sunlight glinting off its ebony feathers. Nantaje shrugged off the feeling and rode on, looking for the narrow slit in the canyon's wall that marked the side canyon where his people had lived in peace for a dozen years.

He found the place and turned onto a well-trodden trail. Canyon walls squeezed in on either side, shooting skyward to a jagged slit of blue far overhead. Slowly the side canyon widened, turning and dividing, and dividing again. Then a sharp bend opened onto a wide amphitheater of about fifty acres. Nantaje reined in at the sight of the lodges set about in an orderly fashion with smoke rising from a dozen cook fires. Women busily worked outside the doors of their wickiups or tended goats as children scampered about, playing. There were a couple of men gathered around the horse corral, but few others in camp at the moment. The sight lifted his spirits and he forgot the nagging worry that had accompanied him all the way down from Fort Bowie.

He clucked his horse forward. When they spotted him, four or five of the children ran to greet him, but as he drew closer and they recognized who it was, the adults sharply called them back. Nantaje grimaced. It was as he suspected. He halted just outside the village and waited as Gato, the village chief, came out to speak to him.

"You have come back, Nantaje," the chief said.

"The army says the wars are over. General Crook has left the land. General Miles has taken his place. Miles has no more use for scouts."

Gato nodded. "I have heard word of this. Come, we will talk."

Nantaje dismounted and the two men walked to a grove of cottonwood trees standing alongside a spring where water gathered in a pool. He quenched his thirst.

"Tell me of Geronimo," Gato said. Gato was a sinewy warrior, not many years older than Nantaje. He had led his people well, keeping them safe here in this isolated canyon, yet still managing to supply their needs. Some called him Cow Thief. His fame for rustling cattle from the surrounding rancherias was legendary among the Apache people.

"He still evades the army, but not for long. His family, and all Chiricahuas on the reservation, have already been put in railroad cars and sent far to the east, to a place called Florida. If Geronimo is captured, he will be sent far away, too."

Gato frowned. "That's not good. The Apache cannot live long separated from the land. It will be better for Geronimo to die here."

"Perhaps. But it is the way of things now. Soon all the Mimbres and Chiricahuas will be captured and forced onto reservations. The army has taken all the strong war chiefs, all except for Geronimo."

"Yet you helped them," Gato noted, raising his dark eyebrows.

"Our people have been at peace with the white man. We have not sought their blood as the Mimbres and Chiricahuas have."

Gato scoffed. "If he has his way, the white man would put us on the reservations, too."

"Maybe it is so. We can only wait and see, Gato. We had a strong ally with Crook. But now that he is gone . . ." Nantaje shrugged, silently shaking his head.

After a moment Gato said, "Not all the people agree that we should not have fought. There is much anger toward the whites in the camp. Many of our warriors ride to fight the white soldiers."

"This is not good. The white are strong, and the Apache have become small in numbers."

"Yet Geronimo has many strong voices here among our people."

Nantaje nodded. "I know that. I will not stay if that is what the people want. But I wish to see my sister and her husband, and little Tejon."

Nantaje took his horse to the common corral and let it run with the others.

"Are you back to stay, Nantaje?" a friend asked as he strode through the village.

"I do not know yet, Nalda," he said. "I will decide after I speak with Turi and Jakinda."

"We must talk later, after you have seen your family."

"Yes, later."

Jakinda was waiting for Nantaje in front of one of the brush and hide wickiups. She set aside the basket from her lap and rose to her feet as he drew near.

"For many seasons I have waited for your return, Nantaje," she said, taking his hands and looking up into his smiling eyes.

"It is good to be back. But my heart is heavy. Gato tells me many of the men are making war."

She frowned. "There is no love between our people and the Chiricahuas, but the warriors go anyway. They see it as a choice between Geronimo or the whites. At least with the Chiricahuas we keep our land."

"And we may yet remain on the land with the white soldiers. Crook wanted it so."

"You are too hopeful, my brother. I think not."

This wasn't a conversation he cared to continue. "Tell me of Tejon. Has he grown tall?"

Her somberness turned to enthusiasm. "He is tall, like his father, like his uncle. He will be a strong warrior one day."

Nantaje glanced around the encampment with sudden concern cutting into his forehead.

"What is it?" Jakinda asked.

"Turi. He is not here."

She smiled, understanding his concern. "You need not worry. He did not go with the warriors. He and Tejon are away hunting. They will be back soon."

Nantaje was relieved to hear that, but his concern still remained, a lingering annoyance, like a thorn buried deep in his skin. It was that same feeling he'd known coming here, and try as he might, he couldn't shake it.

The snap of a twig jarred John Keane from a troubled sleep. Old habits died hard, especially those drilled deep into the soul. Keane did not move at once, but lay motionless upon the tick mattress, listening, his eyes probing the shadows of the cabin, his ears suddenly wary, hearing every sound beyond the open window.

An owl hooted; a coyote howled far off in the distance. . . .

There it was again.

Keane slipped off the bed and crouched beneath the window where a faint breeze moved the ragged cotton curtains. Slowly, silently, he levered the bolt of his Winchester half a stroke. The dull gleam of brass peeked out of the chamber. Closing the breech on the .44, Keane hooked a thumb over the hammer and peered past the corner of the window.

Apache, he thought at first. No. Apaches would not have given themselves away so easily. Whites? Probably. Mexicans maybe. With military precision, Keane ran down the list of possibilities. Scattered clouds obscured the faint light of a crescent moon, and the mountainside beyond the pile of stones and scattered creosote hummocks was black and impenetrable.

15

Gravel clattered softly and a shadow moved.

Keane caught his breath, trying to locate them by sound alone. Three . . . no, four. Two left, two right. He hitched his way across the floor and felt for the box of cartridges on the tabletop. Back at the window, he pumped four cartridges into the magazine, replacing the ones he had used the day before in bringing down a deer.

They had stopped moving now. Keane waited. A stone shifted, clacking softly against another.

"Who's out there?"

A moment passed as the chill night air gently moved the curtains, stroking his face.

"Señor Keane, you are awake?"

Mexican.

"I am now. What the hell do you want, sneaking around my place in the middle of the night?"

"We hear you have silver."

"Well, you hear wrong. Now get out." Keane had the speaker's location pegged—to the right and about ten yards out, hidden behind a stand of mesquite.

"There is the mine, and all this rubble," another voice noted. "Yet you say there is no silver?"

Keane's view shifted to the left. "What's your name?"

"My name is not important," the second man replied. "Give us the silver and we will leave in peace."

"It's a worthless hole, *amigo.* There is no silver. Nothing worth dying for. Now get out of here." Keane held back the trigger and soundlessly thumbed the hammer to full cock. He didn't really expect them to leave so easily, but their words gave away their positions. The longer he could keep them talking, the better.

"I think not, señor. I think there is silver. If you do not give it over, then we will have to take it from you. Then it will be you who will die."

Hunched low, Keane crept across the small cabin and settled beneath the other window, listening.

"What will it be señor?" the man demanded.

The underbelly of a cloud was beginning to brighten. In another minute it would drift out from beneath the moon. "Give me time to think," Keane said, stalling. There was movement again. They were repositioning themselves. Footsteps padded softly near the corner of his cabin. Keane crossed the floor in three strides and hauled aside a barrel of stale bread. Beneath it was a hole in the floor; a tight fit for a man Keane's size, but he squeezed through it and was beneath the cabin.

He lay there listening, watching. A pair of boots appeared at the back corner of the cabin. Keane started toward them, elbowing his way, bare toes digging against the ground, finding every sharp rock, cactus needle, and pointed stick there. Floor joists pressed hard against his back; he expelled the air in his lungs and passed beneath them.

"What have you decided, Señor Keane?" the first Mexican called out. The man hunkered down by the corner began creeping toward the front of the cabin.

Keane wormed his way to the back of the cabin, then was free of it, rolling out and crawling behind the rain barrel. He scrambled to his feet and made a quick dash through the shadows, drawing up behind the privy.

The clouds parted and a pale glow spread across the barren, hard-worked ground.

"Señor Keane, I need your answer now."

"Come and get me, you son of a bitch," Keane whispered, poking his head past the corner of the outhouse and scanning the dark land. The military part of his brain had taken over. High ground lay to the east, climbing steeply from the cabin. From up there he could flank them. It offered an elevated vantage point with good cover.

"Señor, why you no speak?"

Keane held his position, waiting. "Come on . . . come on, make your move," he said beneath his breath, his eyes straining at the blackness where the Mexicans were hiding.

"No more talking, Señor Keane. You have had your chance."

Gunfire shattered the night stillness; muzzle flashes blossomed orange-red from four different points, marking the men's locations. They would be momentarily blinded by that, and Keane used the opportunity to his advantage. Ignoring the pain in his feet, he sprinted up the rise and dove behind a stand of rocks there.

The bullets ripped through the dried boards of his cabin as if it had been made of pasteboard. The Mexicans kept up the fire until it seemed as though a whole battalion had descended on his place. Finally the leader called for a cease-fire and the night fell silent again.

"He is dead, Diego. He has to be. No one could have survived that."

"*Sí.* Take a look, Pablo," Diego ordered, hurriedly feeding cartridges into his Winchester. One of the men crouched toward the cabin. He stopped, listened, then drove a boot into the latch, ripping it from the jamb and slamming the door open. He plunged through as the others drifted out of the darkness and gathered in the moonlight in front of the cabin.

"He is gone, Diego! He is not here!" The one called Pablo appeared in the doorway, concern plain upon his face even in the thin, shifting moonlight. "Where could he have gone?" A note of panic edged his voice.

"Gone? Impossible."

While he still had the element of surprise on his side, Keane set his sights on the Mexican and squeezed the trigger. The rifle boomed and Diego lurched back, gun flying into the shadows. The others dove for cover, and as the glare of the rifle shot left his eyes Keane spied one of them scrambling behind his woodpile. Pablo was still in the cabin. He'd lost the fourth man.

"Where is he?" someone asked.

"Shut up!" another barked.

"Diego is down."

"Up there somewhere. I saw the flash of his muzzle when he fired."

Patience was the key to a battle like this, and when he had to be, Keane was a man with the cool endurance of a cat. He waited, surveying the dark landscape with the deadly determination of a man who had fought against the odds before, and had won.

A splash of moonlight glinted off the shirtsleeve of the one behind the wood. But it would be a difficult shot and the man wasn't going anywhere—not without Keane seeing him. Pablo was still inside the cabin, but because the night was so dark, Keane figured it was unlikely the Mexican would discover the hole in the floor—a trapdoor Keane had made with Apaches in mind. Diego was down and not moving. Where was the fourth man?

A long breath helped calm him. He let it out slowly. Gunfire still rang in his ears and he strained to hear the sounds around him. His eyes were in constant motion, trying to see everywhere at once. Suddenly the man behind the wood sprinted into the open, rushing for the back of the cabin. Keane snapped the rifle over and fired. The man stumbled and plunged headlong into the shadows.

His shot gave away his position, and gunfire exploded from the cabin and from someplace beyond. Keane drew himself tight against the rock as bullets splattered around him. When it stopped, he swung out and snapped off a shot, then rolled across the ground and flattened himself behind the trunk of a creosote tree. As fast as he could work the lever he sent six bullets slamming into the cabin.

The night grew quiet again. Keane waited, listening. Somewhere far to his left a horse whinnied. The pounding of hooves briefly broke the silence; then all was quiet again. For five minutes nothing moved below. Keane circled his claim and came up behind the woodpile. Not far away lay the dead man. Keeping to the shadows, Keane soundlessly sidled alongside his cabin, listening. Working his way under it again to the escape hole, he slowly poked his head up through the floor.

Not six inches away a face stared back at him. Keane froze; then he realized the eyes were those of a dead man, with a bloody hole between them. Keane shuddered, then pulled himself into the cabin. The place was in shambles, with moonlight streaming in from two dozen holes. Broken dishes littered the floor everywhere. Bullets had shredded his bedding and shattered lamps. The smell of coal oil was thick in the air.

Outside, Keane bent over the one called Diego. He was still breathing. Keane kicked the man's revolver aside, turned him over, and lifted his head. Diego was a young man, not much past his teens. His eyes fluttered open and he looked up at him. A faint grin slowly shaped itself upon his dark face.

"Señor," he said, his voice harsh, breathy, "you are a sly one, like the fox, yes?"

"You should have left when you had the chance."

"I . . . I did not think one man could fight four and live. I have heard of your skill, señor. I think maybe it is all big words? I was wrong."

"Sort of looks that way."

"The others? My brothers?"

"Two dead. One got away."

Diego smiled and nodded. "Good. Then he will return with the others. You should have given us the silver, Señor Keane. My family, they will have their revenge; this I promise you." Diego coughed, bringing up a red froth.

Keane shook his head. "I told you the truth. There is no silver. The mine is worthless. Nothing but a dry hole, my friend. I was planning to pull up stakes and leave it anyway. You and your brothers died for nothing."

Disbelief momentarily flooded Diego's face, swept away in an instant by a racking cough that left the Mexican staring blindly up at the dark, drifting clouds and fleeting moonlight.

Keane lowered the man's head to the ground and limped to the splintered door of his riddled cabin. He sat there a long while in nothing but his long johns, shaking now that the battle was over. Slowly he became aware of the fire in his feet. He looked at the blood and grimaced, and set about the task of removing cactus needles from them.

Chapter Two

A raw piece of civilization carved out of a burning Arizona desert, Tombstone was fit only for rattlesnakes and Apache. It was a blend of clapboard buildings and coarse adobe mud that at first sight appeared to stagger drunkenly along Allen Street as if they had been thrown up with no plan in mind. And afterward, when more people began moving in, whatever space was left between them wider than the span of a dead man, was filled with another shack serving up bad whiskey, marked cards, and soiled doves.

Tombstone's only excuse for existing was silver, and some of the mines were paying off very well indeed. But it was the sporting ladies who mainly attracted men off their claims and into dark back-room cribs. Come morning, the alleyways always had at least one dead man to serve up for breakfast.

Keane rode up Allen Street trailing his morning shadow and leading three horses. The bodies tied over their saddles caused only casual glances from this town so accustomed to death. He reined up in front of the new courthouse just as Deputy Hank Rader was coming out the door. Rader stood on the top step as Keane swung down.

"They told me I'd find you here, Hank."

"What happened, John?"

"These three yahoos and a fourth one jumped my claim last night. Seems someone is talking it up that I made a big strike. They figured on making a withdrawal."

Rader frowned. "You did all three of them?"

"Didn't have much choice."

"How'd you manage it?"

Keane grimaced. "Pretended I was fighting the Apaches again and treated them as such."

"And the fourth one?"

"Got away, and I didn't feel like running him down. Do you know them?" Keane swung off his horse.

Rader came down the steps and lifted one of the heads by its coarse, black hair. "Rodolfo Ortega. Heard he killed a man down in Fronteras. The Mexican authorities are looking for this one." He moved on. "Ah! Diego Ortega. I've a warrant on him in my office. Killed two miners over in the Patagonia district last year. And Pablo Ortega. No paper on this one far as I know, but there ought to be." Rader let the head fall back. "There might be some reward money in this for you, John."

"Not interested in any reward, Hank. Your taking them off my hands will be payment enough."

"I'll see that the undertaker gets 'em. What do you know about the one who got away?"

"A brother. Diego spoke a few words before dying."

"Hmm. That would be either Porfirio or Tomás. Too bad he got away. Either one makes for a bad enemy."

"So Diego told me."

"I'd listen to his words. Watch yourself."

"I always do. If you need me I'll be over at Caesar's Coffeehouse getting something to eat." Keane put the horses with their burden of dead into the deputy's hand and began to lead his own horse away.

"What's wrong with you, John?"

"Wrong?"

You're walking like you got yourself a boot full of cactus needles."

Keane gave a short laugh. "More truth to that than you might reckon, Hank."

Up the street a stagecoach was disgorging itself of army officers and their wives, bound for Camp Huachuca. Keane didn't recognize any of them, but he steered clear of the stage just the same, pausing a while in the mouth of an alleyway where excited miners were making bets on the outcome of a cockfight. The roosters clawed themselves ragged in a whirlwind of dust and feathers and blood until finally the men broke up what was left of them. A winner was declared and money changed hands. By then the stage had pulled away toward the livery and the soldiers had dispersed. The heat of the day was growing as Keane crossed the dusty street to Caesar's Coffeehouse and stepped from harsh sunlight into the cool darkness of the eatery.

The place wasn't fancy, but it was clean by Tombstone standards. Keane stood just inside the door a moment while his eyes adjusted. It was a long, narrow building with a low ceiling and a packed-earth floor. The only light came from two small front windows. Six or seven pine tables were scattered about, and five men sat at three of them. Two soldiers chatted quietly up front near the windows. The banker, Jenkins, was taking a late breakfast at another. Two men had the third table at the back, playing cards and drinking coffee.

Keane tried not to let the misery in his feet show as he crossed to a vacant table and leaned his Winchester against the wall. It was a good place to keep an eye on the door. Not that he was expecting trouble. Leastwise, not so soon.

"Morning, Mr. Keane. Ain't seen you in town for a while. That mine of yours must been keeping you busy."

Laura Caesar was a plump, middle-aged woman with a friendly smile and a fierce curiosity about everything going on around Tombstone. If there was gossip to be had, Laura was sure to be one of its main dispensers. Keane never told her anything he wanted to keep private. It would be like announcing it from the stage of the Bird Cage Theater. She'd come with a cup and a pot of hot coffee, as if she knew exactly what he needed.

"I don't get in much these days," he said. "But eventually the beans and flour run out."

"Living like you do, all by yourself out there, is going to turn you into a lonely old man. You need to be around folks more."

He grinned. "No, thanks. Spent plenty of time doing the social thing. I kind of like my own company . . . at least for now."

Her blue eyes brightened. "Oh, really? And just what was it you did before coming to dig silver, Mr. Keane?"

Laura was scratching for some interesting tidbit of his past, something to make its way like wildfire first through St. Paul's Episcopal Church and then the whole town. His smile widened and he said, "I'll have a slice of beef, well done, a few eggs, and fry me up some potatoes, but hold the chilies."

Running up against his blockade, Laura moved off, refilling coffee cups as she headed back toward the kitchen door. Keane stretched his legs out under the table, taking some pressure off the tender spots on the soles of his feet. Heat had begun to work its way through the walls and roof. The soldiers left, and Keane's thoughts briefly slipped back to the time he wore blue and carried a saber. It had been a hard life, but most rewarding to a man of his nature. A scowl shaped itself upon his face when he recalled how it had ended. Laura was looking at him curiously. He grinned at her. She scurried into the kitchen. Keane's attention was drawn to the two men playing cards.

One of the men was older, maybe his own age, late forties. His face was sharp-featured and clean shaven. His hat lay on a vacant chair and his dark hair was shot through with gray. Keane studied him, his bearing, his emotionless face, and figured him for a gambler. Then the other man shifted upon his chair and Keane saw that the gambler had only one arm. An ex-military man, Keane decided. He had the bearing that spoke of officer training, and the missing right arm spoke of the rebellion now twenty years past.

"Thank you, suh. Ah will take two," the gambler said in a soft Southern voice, collecting the cards and expertly arranging them one-handedly among the others.

Confederate, Keane figured. He held no particular bitterness toward the South or her soldiers. They had fought valiantly and they had lost—lost not because of the caliber of her officers or the bravery of her young men. It had been a war mainly of economics, and the North had held all the trump cards. Just the same, the conflict had been bitterly waged, and many still nursed the deep wounds it had left. Keane had been a lieutenant when the first shots had been fired across Charleston Harbor, and a brevetted colonel by the time Lee surrendered to Grant four years later.

Keane's breakfast came. Laura refilled his coffee cup and he turned his attention to the meal, half his brain keeping track of what was happening in the small eatery around him while the other half pondered the Ortegas, weighing what his next move should be. He wondered where they had gotten the notion that he had struck it big. Maybe they were only guessing. Or maybe someone was spreading rumors. He grinned and glanced at Laura making her rounds with the coffeepot. Not Laura Caesar. He had never made any pretenses around her.

"See here, Louvel! Where did that card come from?" the

man said in a growl, staring hard and accusingly at the gambler. Jenkins, over at his table, lowered his copy of the *Nugget* and peered curiously at the two cardplayers. The chair scraped hard against the floor and the man stood. He was a big-shouldered gent with the bulging arms of a miner. He stood nearly six-four and wore a dangerous snarl that matched the threatening tone in his voice. A revolver was stuck in his belt, and now the man's hand moved toward it. Keane put down his fork and measured up the situation. The one-armed man would be no match if push came to shove.

The Southerner remained unruffled. He slowly put his cards on the table facedown and placed his hand atop them. "You just dealt it to me, suh," he replied easily with his dark eyes locked on the big fellow. Steady, unflinching eyes they were. Black like an Apache's, showing him for a man who would not easily give ground.

"Yeah, and my little old Aunt Betsy is a spike driver for the Union Pacific, too."

"Are you calling me a liar?"

Keane had to strain to hear the words.

"I am, Louvel. I'm saying you had an extra ace hid somewhere and you switched 'em. Don't know how you did it, cripple, but you did. Not only are you a liar, but you're a damned cheat, too. What do you intend to do about it, One-Arm?"

The one-armed man kicked the table away, slamming it into the man, knocking him off balance. He leaped around it, swinging his left fist hard into the fellow's chin. The smack resounded in the small café. Keane winced as if it had been his jaw that had taken the blow and scrambled out of the way as the man reeled into his table, sending his breakfast to the floor.

"Damn your miserable hide!" the miner said with a growl, plowing back into the Southerner. The one-armed man was of light build and no more than five-ten or -eleven, but he was quick as a jackrabbit on hot sand, and his fist struck, recoiled, and struck again with rattlesnake precision. The man had a sense about him, as if he intuitively knew where the next punch was going to come from, and anticipating it, he somehow managed to keep just beyond it.

Two men had just entered the café. They leaped aside as the big man backpedaled out into the street with the Southerner, tenacious as a bulldog, right after him. Keane and the others scrambled out into the heat after them.

They circled each other at first, a little like those cocks Keane had watched earlier; then the miner lunged. He was fast for his bulk and for the first time the gambler miscalculated. He took it low, in the stomach, and his breath exploded from him. The two of them rolled in the dirt, thrashing and clawing and lifting a whirlwind of dust beneath the burning Arizona sun.

Not only did the miner have bulk to his advantage, he was a good ten years younger. But for all his disadvantage, the one-armed man was holding his own remarkably well. They tumbled into the hitch rail and the horses danced and strained at their reins to keep away from the two combatants. Then the gambler landed a knee in the other's groin and sent him howling into the middle of Allen Street.

Bleeding and unsteady, the gambler got to his feet. He was breathing heavily and sweating hard, but there was still plenty of fight left in those black eyes of his. He was a tough bird. Keane was impressed.

"Suh," he said, drawing in a long breath, "you have sullied my clothes and my reputation. Ah will accept your apology now."

Groaning softly, the miner glared back with hate in his eyes. "And you shall get it in hell, you son of a bitch!" His hand stabbed for the revolver tucked under his belt.

The gambler didn't move right away, and by the time he did, the other man already had his gun drawn and was thumbing back the hammer. The gambler had started for something inside his coat, but he was way behind the miner's draw. Instinctively, Keane's hand swept down for his Colt. It came out smooth and fast. He was a heartbeat behind the miner, but the man was hurting and he took an instant to steady his aim.

Keane's revolver roared and the miner's gun spun away into the dirt.

The miner let out a cry and grabbed his wrist, blood seeping through his fingers. By this time the gambler had his pistol out, a small Remington Derringer, but by then it was all over. The marshal came sprinting over with a scattergun in one hand.

"All right, someone had better do some talking here," the marshal ordered. He spied Keane and the Colt he was holding. "You've been having yourself quite a spree, haven't you?"

Keane holstered the gun. "I see you have talked to your deputy."

"What happened here?"

Before Keane could answer, the gambler spoke up. "The gentleman on the ground took offense at losing at cards, suh. He called me a cheat. Ah gave him some basic instructions on manners. Apparently not taking well to his lessons, he reached for his gun. Ah was a bit slow, or Ah would have furthered his education on marksmanship. As it is, he is fortunate Ah hesitated. This gentleman stepped in, and to him Ah am indebted." The Southerner turned toward Keane and bent slightly at the waist.

The marshal frowned and snatched the revolver off the street. "Anyone here who can verify that is what happened?"

"I can, Marshal," Jenkins said.

The lawman nodded. "Your word is good with me." He hauled the miner up and said, "All right, big fellow. Let's go find the doc and have him look at that hand. Then there's a cot waiting for you in a cell."

"But he cheated! He had to have!"

The marshal peered at the gambler. "Don't see how he could have, not with one of his wings missing like it is."

"Some men mistake skill for double-dealing. Ah assure you, Ah do not cheat." He slipped the pistol back into his inside pocket and slapped the dust from his clothing. The crowd broke up and Keane started back to survey the damage to his breakfast.

"Suh."

Keane looked back.

"Thank you for stepping forward."

"Forget it."

"It was not necessary, you understand. Ah could have finished off the rascal myself."

Keane lifted his eyebrows. "Oh, could you, now? Looked to me like he had you dead in his sights."

"He would have missed me with his first shot. And Ah would not have permitted a second."

The man was arrogant. Keane had no interest in arguing the point with him. "Maybe you're right." He turned back to the café.

"Of course Ah am right. The gun was shaking like a leaf."

Keane stopped inside the doorway and surveyed the ruined café. Laura was busily righting tables, and her kitchen help, an old Mexican man in a filthy apron, was gathering up dishes, picking the good ones from among the shattered glass. Keane frowned. Laura would have made good on the meal, but he'd lost his appetite. He'd killed three men the day before, and shot a fourth today. As the marshal had said, he was on quite a spree. He went inside for his rifle.

The Southerner was still standing there when Keane limped toward his horse.

"Ah will be pleased to buy you a drink, suh."

Keane looked over the curve of his saddle at the man. He didn't think he liked him very much. His arrogance chafed, and there was something in his dark eyes that made his skin crawl. But right then a drink sounded mighty good. It had been years since he'd shared a bottle with another man, but that had been his own choosing. He squinted up at the burning sky, then at the dark doorway down the street, and nodded. "All right, friend. I'll drink with you."

They left their horses tied there and strode side by side. Keane stood half a head taller than the one-armed man, but the man walked a brisk pace, as if the fight were no more than a distant memory. Maybe it was the ache in his own feet that made Keane notice that.

"My name is Royden Louvel."

"John Keane."

"Are you from this godforsaken land, sir?"

Keane laughed. "Is any white man from this country? I've moved around a lot, Mr. Louvel. But I've been in the area about three years now."

They stepped up to the boardwalk and into the cooler air of the saloon. Louvel paid for a bottle and carried it to a table. Keane set his rifle on the table with it and waited for the Southerner to fill their glasses.

"To moving around, Mr. Keane," he said, lifting his glass.

Keane clinked his against his host's and took a long swallow. The raw whiskey burned clear down to his belly.

"Ah've moved around a lot, too," Louvel said. "The pattern of my life for quite some years now."

"From what part of the South do you hail?"

"New Orleans. Ah am of the New Orleans Louvels, suh. And yourself?"

"Ohio. Least, that's where I was born. Left when I was sixteen." He grinned. "I heard that far-off call to adventure, and I've been looking for her ever since."

Louvel didn't smile. Keane figured that, like his right arm, he had lost his sense of humor, too. He was uncom-

Jason Elder

fortable drinking with the man and itched to be getting back to his claim.

"Ohio, you say?" He studied Keane. "You are old enough to have fought."

Keane frowned. "I am, and I did. And so did you, I'd guess. That is where you lost the arm."

"You are correct, suh. The Battle of Gaines's Mill. Lee proved his mettle in that one." Louvel's face hardened. "But our casualties were staggering. Over eighty-seven hundred men. Many friends, many splendid officers."

"I thought I detected the bearing of a military man in you."

"West Point, suh. Class of fifty-eight. Ah was a captain in sixty-two when Ah lost this." He raised his stump slightly. "And you, suh?"

"That was a long time ago."

"Twenty-four years, if you care to count. Ah've stopped, yet it seems like only last week. Who was your officer in command? Perhaps Ah know of him?"

Keane didn't like the course their conversation had taken. He didn't particularly like Louvel either. The man was caught up in the past, a past Keane had already put behind him. He finished his drink and stood. "Thank you for the whiskey, Mr. Louvel, and the conversation, but I've got to be going."

"Ah asked you a question."

Keane bristled at his demanding tone, but he remained unmoved on the outside. "My commanding officer was Rutherford B. Hayes, of the Twenty-third Ohio. And if it makes any difference, like yourself, I was a captain at the time."

"A Yankee! Ah suspected as much."

"We lost a lot of good men and officers, too."

"And we our land, our country."

"It was an honorable surrender, Mr. Louvel. Grant gave Lee the most generous concessions he could."

32

"We are a sovereign country presently occupied by a foreign government, and there is nothing going to change that short of another bloody rebellion!"

Now Keane was certain he didn't like Louvel. "Well, sir, you can go right on fighting your war if you want to. For me it ended in sixty-five." He grabbed his rifle and strode out into the Arizona sun. Shoving a boot into the stirrup, he swung onto his horse and started back to his hardscrabble mine and shot-up cabin.

Chapter Three

Turi and Tejon returned that evening with a young doe hanging from a pole between them. It had been two years since Nantaje had seen his brother-in-law and nephew, and he was amazed at how much Tejon had grown.

"You are nearly the size of a warrior!" he declared, clasping the boy on the shoulders and looking him over.

Tejon grinned.

"He killed the doe," Turi said, not trying to hide the pride he felt toward his son. "I am surprised to see you here, Nantaje. Come, we will talk. You will tell me about the white soldiers, and of Geronimo. Is it true that he will finally make peace?"

"I do not think so, not yet at least. But he cannot hold out against General Miles's soldiers much longer." The two men strolled toward the stream that wound its way down the canyon, relishing the coolness of the coming evening.

"Why are you not with them?"

Nantaje frowned. "They say there is no more need for

Apache scouts. General Crook is gone and General Miles is sending most of the Apache home." Nantaje shook his head. "But without the Apache, Miles will not easily root out Geronimo."

"There are many here in the village who want to see Geronimo keep fighting."

"Yes, Gato has said this. Some of the young warriors have already gone to fight with him."

They stopped by the stream and Turi stooped to scoop a handful of water to his mouth. "Some resent the scouts who led the white soldiers," he said, wiping his chin.

"I do not know if I will stay long, Turi. But I wanted to see you, and Tejon, and my sister before going."

"Going? Where would you go?"

"I don't know. Maybe Mexico."

"Many of our people have fled to Mexico. But there is no safety there where we still have many enemies."

Nantaje and Turi started back toward the village. Suddenly Nantaje stopped and looked around.

"What is it?" Turi asked.

The scout's eyes narrowed, shifting to the rocky cliffs hemming in the little village. "I do not know." He scoured the tawny landscape, then shivered. A pair of ravens took flight and circled, calling angrily before winging out over the canyon wall and disappearing. "Listen."

"I hear nothing."

Nantaje nodded, as if that only confirmed his suspicions. "I have felt something ever since riding away from Fort Bowie yesterday."

"What?"

He thought, then managed a grin. "As the white man might say, it is an itch I can't quite scratch."

Turi looked at him curiously, plainly not understanding its meaning.

More nervous now, Nantaje said, "Let's get back to the village."

"You have lived among the whites too long," Turi chided.

"Yes, and it is not an experience I would wish upon my worst enemy."

Turi lifted a questioning eyebrow. "Another white man's saying?"

He grinned. "You are right. I *have* lived among the white men too long. But I have come away with much. I have tried to learn what they could teach me, even though they were not aware of doing so."

"You have always been clever, Nantaje. I wonder sometimes how you do it."

"By keeping my eyes and ears open, and my mouth shut."

All at once the crack of a rifle echoed off the canyon walls. A .45-70 Springfield—Nantaje recognized it immediately. He flinched, and the same instant Turi lurched forward and slammed into the ground. Suddenly a volley of rifle fire crashed in on the village.

Nantaje threw himself to the ground and rolled behind a low hummock of coarse buffalo grass. In the village, women were dashing for cover, grabbing up little children in their arms while the few warriors who remained in camp made a scramble for cover to make a stand. Gunfire from their hidden attackers cut them down. Nantaje tried to spot them, but spied only the rising smoke from their weapons ranging along the rocks ahead.

He leaped to his feet and ran a zigzagging course toward the wickiups as bullets kicked up spits of dust at his feet. He dove behind one of the lodges and crawled to his sister's lodge. Tejon was crouched in the doorway, protecting it with a war lance. Nantaje pushed passed him and found Jakinda inside, wide-eyed, fear etched in her face.

"Turi?" she asked, panic rising in her voice. "Where is Turi?"

Nantaje cast about for some kind of weapon. The only

thing at hand was Turi's bow and a few arrows in his quiver. His people had no quarrel with the white man and had not prepared for war. Now, with most of the warriors away aiding Geronimo, and the rest lying dead or bleeding, their situation looked hopeless.

"Where is my husband?"

He shot a glance at her. "Turi is dead."

"No!"

"Has he more arrows somewhere?"

Tejon was staring in through the doorway, his face drawn tight, shock showing in his young eyes. He had heard.

"Arrows!" Nantaje demanded. "Are there any more?"

There came the pounding of hooves from outside. Tejon leaped inside just as a horse rushed by. Others swept past. The reports of rifles gave way to the sharp crack of revolvers. Women and children cried out in terror, trying to flee, but Nantaje knew the situation was hopeless. A horse drew to a stop outside and a man dressed in army blue and brandishing a Colt revolver stuck his head inside and pointed the weapon.

Nantaje scrambled in front of his sister, putting himself between her and the gun.

"Hold up there, buck," the soldier ordered. "Make one move for that bow and I'll drill ya."

Nantaje raised his hands. "You are making a mistake. We are White Mountain Apache."

"You talk pretty good American for an Injun. It's no mistake. Crawl out of there now, and be quick about it." He backed out of the way.

Outside, people were being herded together; women, children, those men who had survived the first wave of the attack. Men in blue had ringed themselves around the village. At first Nantaje thought there were more of them, but he counted only seven. They were ill-kempt, and their uniforms had seen better days. Unlike the soldiers he was used to, these men seemed to lack discipline, and for the most part it had been days, if not weeks, since any of them had touched a razor or a bar of soap.

They lined the people along one edge of the village while two men rode out to check on the bodies sprawled about the camp. A thickset man with the stripes of a sergeant on his blue uniform blouse considered the Apache a moment. Nantaje knew this man, but could not recall his name. It had been many years back. They had both ridden under the command of Major J. R. Keane at the time, but that was all he could remember. He had been assigned to a different company shortly afterward.

The sergeant's eyes fell upon him and a thin smile nudged the corner of his mouth. "I know you. Your name is Nantaje. You did some scouting for us some time ago, didn't you? Miles gave you the boot, did he? There's no honor left in this man's army, is there?"

"We are at peace with the whites. Why have you attacked our village, killed our men?"

"Whatever deal you folks cut with the general, that's between you and him. Me and my boys, we don't work for Uncle Sam no more. You might say we finally got fed up with the United States Army and went out on our own."

"Yeah, we're freelancing," another man put in. The soldiers seemed to find that funny somehow.

Another man rode up. "There's eight of 'em down, Sam." He glanced along the line of frightened women and children, noting the few men interspersed among them. "Not many bucks in this village."

"Where are all the bucks?" the sergeant asked Nantaje.

Now he remembered his name: Butler, Sam Butler. "Most are away. They went to help Geronimo."

"Geronimo, huh? Too bad. Well, reckon it can't be helped now."

"Ortega pays double for the bucks," a man astride his horse next to Butler noted.

"I know that," Butler shot back. "Ortega is gonna have to be satisfied with what we bring him. It'll be easier to handle them this way, and he pays good silver for kids and women, too." Butler turned in the saddle and called to one of the men riding a slow circle around the camp, searching for Apache still in hiding. "Green! Bring up the shackles."

Walt Green reined his horse about and trotted toward the mouth of the valley, where a packhorse waited.

After they snapped the iron cuffs onto the men, not bothering to chain the women, Butler swung out of the saddle and strode in front of them as if inspecting his troops. "Listen up, how many understand English?"

"I only," Nantaje said.

"Then you tell them my words, buck. Tell them I'm taking them on a march of three days. Tell the women to take what food and water they can carry 'cause I ain't feeding them, and there's little to drink where we're going. Tell them I don't expect any trouble, and I don't intend to put up with none."

Nantaje translated the warning.

"Tell them I'll kill every man, woman, and kid here if anyone tries to escape."

He did.

Without warning Butler drew his revolver and fired at a woman standing there. The slug punched her in the chest and knocked her to the ground.

A cry of shocked disbelief ran through the captives as women clutched children closer and men moved to protect their wives. No one spoke, but the fire of revenge burned hot in the warriors' eyes while children began to whimper.

Butler eyed Nantaje and grinned. "Tell them that was just to show I mean what I say. We got us a long march ahead of us." Butler holstered the revolver. "It will be dark soon, so get water and food together and let's move. You, buck," Butler said, glaring at Nantaje. "I expect you to keep your people in line. I ain't fooling around when I say

I'll shoot them all, so don't try me. There are plenty more where these came from."

Nantaje looked at the heavy shackles about his wrists. He had seen similar constraining devices many times before, in the army guard houses, or when the army had transported prisoners. The other warriors were similarly bound; even Gato bore the shame of being a prisoner, captured in his own village. Nantaje could not allow this indignity to go unpunished, could not permit this violence against his people to go unanswered. But for now, at least, he was helpless to do anything but obey, or face death, and the death of all he loved. He glanced at Jakinda with Tejon at her side.

Tejon was almost grown, but just then, huddled there beside his mother with fear upon his young face, he looked every bit the child he still was.

Nantaje told the people to take what they could carry to see them through, for they could expect no mercy at the hands of these renegade soldiers. He'd been warned that the trek would be hard and water scarce, but he was determined to make it to the end, and then somehow, some way, he would see to it that these white men paid for what they had done here!

Butler drove the Apache, and the horses he had stolen from them, all night, permitting them to stop only twice for brief rests to eat and drink. Nantaje had walked at his sister's side most of the way, until one of the older women staggered and stumbled, and he'd rushed to bear her weight upon his shoulder so that she could keep up with the others.

Sometime after three in the morning Nantaje realized they had crossed over into Mexico. The "border." A line drawn upon a map. That was all it meant to him, all it meant to any Indian for whom the concept of actually owning the land was as foreign as owning the sky or the air.

But for the white man, owning was so important they would go to war over lines drawn on paper. Nantaje had lived with the white man for nearly half a dozen years, had learned their language, their sayings, their peculiarities. But even though he knew them, he did not understand them, and he suspected he never would.

A crisp dawn crimsoned the eastern sky, and then daylight spread across the land. The morning wore on, growing hot, and still Butler and his men kept the Indians moving. The direction was all Nantaje knew for sure. They were heading south and west, and he noted the lay of the land, memorizing the landmarks, imprinting them upon his brain so he could find his way back. It was not unfamiliar territory to the Apache scout, but just the same, Nantaje had not spent a lot of time in Mexico, not like some others, like Geronimo or Nana, or even Cochise years before them.

Butler drew rein finally and made a face at the sun, shading his eyes with a hand. "We'll hold up here awhile," he said, noting a cool grove of paloverde below a sharp-stone cliff that threw a swath of shade across the ground. Butler glanced at Nantaje.

"Tell your people they can range out along those rocks and rest. But I'm warning you, anyone tries to run off, me and my men will kill every redskin-bastard one of you." He glanced at one of the men, who had a dusty white shirt open in front and a fine powder of red dust coating his worn blue britches. "Green."

"Sarge?"

"Scout the area. See if you can't find that seep we come across last spring. Need to water the horses."

The soldier rode off and the others dismounted, taking their animals to shade. The Apache remained in the sun, not daring to move until Nantaje told them to find refuge along the rock wall. He passed on Butler's warning, but the women and children weren't about to leave the men, and each of them were shackled in iron. Nantaje looked at his own chain and cuffs, recalling a time a few years earlier when he'd become friends with a jailer in charge of the stockades at Fort Bowie. They'd shared many hours of friendly conversation. Nantaje, as usual, had listened hard and had soaked it all in. He'd learned much from that jailer.

"Have some water, my brother," Jakinda said, bringing the limp drinking bag to him. He hefted it and frowned. "It is all we have left," she said.

Nantaje poured a small amount into his mouth, then twisted the plug back in place and handed it back. "They say there is water somewhere near." Nantaje sniffed the air, studied the land, then grinned. "But he went off in the wrong direction. If there is water, it lies that way." He nodded at a swath of slightly different-colored vegetation not very far away.

Jakinda looked, but did not share his smile. He knew she was thinking of Turi, and was desperately worried about Tejon. They walked to where the others had settled in the shade.

"Maybe it will be better if you do not show me special favors, Jakinda."

"What do you mean?" she asked, her dark eyes searching his face.

"It might be better if they do not know you are my sister, or that Tejon is my nephew."

Her eyes narrowed. "What is it you are thinking?"

"These soldiers are renegades. They are not following the wishes of the white chiefs. What they do, they do for their own reasons. I do not know yet what their plans are, but when the time is right I intend to escape and take word of their location to Captain McGowan. When I do, they might take out their anger on you and Tejon if they know we are related."

"But they said they will kill us all if even one escapes."

"I hear them speak of someone named Ortega, and the

42

money he will pay them. If I know white men like I think I do, as long as they get their money, they will not care if one of us should escape."

She thought this over, then looked at the shackles upon his wrists. "Those will make escape difficult."

He grinned. "Yes, they will. But not for me."

Jakinda cocked her head as if trying to decipher his meaning.

"Don't worry about these chains. For now, treat me as any other man here. When the time comes, I will know it, and it is best that you do not."

She nodded and took the gut water bag to another man, and when he had drunk from it, down the line to the next. Tejon was watching him. The boy started to stand, but the scout gave him a quick shake of his head and a warning look. The boy was smart and did not need to be told twice. He settled back down in the shade and folded his arms upon his knees, resting his weary head upon them. Nantaje strolled a little distance away and found a spot of shade where he could be alone, where he could think and observe . . . and plan.

The renegades had settled in among the paloverde to wait out the heat of the day. Butler uncapped his canteen and took a long drink. Corp. Conrad Gunther hunkered down beside him.

"We've made good time, Sam. If we keep up this pace we could be there tomorrow night."

"Sooner the better. Herding Apache across this desert ain't my idea of fun." Butler slapped the cork into the canteen and set it aside. He fished around inside a canvas bag for a piece of hardtack, clenched it in his teeth, snapped off a corner, and worked it around in his mouth, moistening it.

Gunther lowered himself onto the ground with a soft moan of relief. "Hope Green finds that seep, Sarge. We're running shy of water."

"If not, there's another along the way."

Gunther licked his dry lips. "Horses need it more than we do."

"They'll hold out." Butler glanced at the captive Apache. "Too bad we couldn't catch us some more bucks. Ortega pays double for bucks." Then a slow grin worked its way onto his face. "But there sure are a lot of women." His voice held a wistful note. He glanced at Gunther. "Been a long time since I've had me a woman, Conrad."

Gunther looked over at the weary captives and shook his head. "Been a long time for me, too, but I prefer my females scrubbed and scented, and it's nice if they can talk my own language."

"Hell with talking. And as far as being scrubbed and scented, you ain't much to look at or smell. Take my word on that."

Gunther wiped the sweat from his brow with his sleeve and levered his hat back in place. "Maybe. Too hot for that now."

"There's always later, when the sun goes down."

Walt Green came back not having found the seep they were looking for. "It must have gone dry, is all I can think of," he said discouraged.

The news brought a heightened uneasiness among the renegades, and tempers were on edge. From his place in the lengthening shade near the cliffs, Nantaje grinned. He knew where the water lay. He could almost smell it, yet these white men might walk their horses over the place a dozen times and never know what lay just inches beneath the hard earth. As yet, his people were not suffering from lack of water, so he saw no compelling reason to tell Butler.

Peter Hennigan laughed and said, "Green has problems finding his own pecker in the dark."

Green wheeled, his fists bunched and ready. "You're asking to have your nose busted!"

It was too hot to fight, so Hennigan dragged out his

revolver and laid it casually across his lap. "Come give it your best shot, Green."

Jon Setter broke it up, said he'd search out the seep for a while, and strode off. He came back an hour or two later with the same story. It had been seasonal and was dry for the summer. But there was water ahead and they had to content themselves with that, and hope it too wasn't a seasonal thing.

They napped the rest of the afternoon, played cards, and discussed what they were going to do once they had turned Nantaje's people over to Ortega. When the sun dipped toward the west and the heat began to retreat off the land, Butler roused his men and herded the Apache back into a line. He made a head count. Once he was satisfied they were all there, they resumed their southwesterly march.

Chapter Four

The old woman was having trouble. Even with Nantaje walking at her side, bearing some of her weight, she was falling behind.

"That squaw is slowing us down," Butler said to one of the men, called Bitter Johnson. Before he had known the man's name, Nantaje had thought of him as "Tall Drink of Water." It was a white man's expression, one of the hundreds he'd learned living with them, and it seemed to fit the man. Bitter Johnson was about six feet, five inches tall and no thicker around the middle than an old snubbing post. When he walked it was in long, easy strides, his arms swinging like lazy pendulums at his sides, hands flapping at the wrists like small pennants.

Johnson glanced at the sergeant, his sharp features a confusion of chalky angles in the moonlight. "Ortega won't want her, Sam. Unnecessary baggage is all she is."

"He's right," Setter put in, riding on Butler's left and a little behind. "Ortega wants 'em young and strong."

Butler turned and looked at the Apache. Nantaje couldn't make out his expression in the dark. "Maybe you're right, boys. Maybe we'd be better off dumping her."

"She's just slowing us down," Johnson said.

Butler nodded, drew rein, and turned his horse to face the Indians. Gunther and Hennigan were at the rear of the column herding the Indian ponies. They drew up as well. Green and a man named Jimmy Caulder rode a few hundred feet ahead, picking out the trail.

"Pull her out of line," Butler ordered Nantaje.

"I will help her. She will not delay you," Nantaje said.

"She ain't worth the bother, buck. I said pull her out of line!" Butler's gun snapped up, its hammer clicking back.

"You will leave her and not harm her?"

Butler grinned. "Sure, we'll just leave her. She's Apache, ain't she? She can make her way out of here with no trouble."

Nantaje could never trust these men, but they left him no choice. Gently he explained what was happening as he guided the old woman away from the others. She nodded and put out a hand to steady herself against a rock.

"Now, get back in line," Butler ordered.

"We must leave her with some food."

"No. No food!"

Reluctantly, Nantaje joined the others. They began moving again. His heart went out to her. Suddenly the hair at the back of his neck began to rise. He looked quickly at Butler and saw the signal the renegade had just passed back to the men at the rear. Hennigan was unbuttoning his holster flap and drawing out his revolver.

Nantaje reached down for a rock the size of a gourd. "No!" he cried.

Hennigan glanced over.

At Fort Bowie, Nantaje had become a solid infielder for the Second Cavalry's Troop B baseball club, standing in as

a pitcher whenever Corporal Miller was out doing guard
duty. As a boy he had played a similar game of pitching
rocks and hitting them with sticks. He'd been good at it
and the white man's baseball had come naturally to him.
Now Hennigan's gun seemed to take the shape of a bat in
the hands of one of Troop I's hard hitters.

Winding up, Nantaje let the rock fly. It smacked the
revolver dead-on and it discharged into the ground at the
old woman's feet.

"Run!" he shouted. Johnson and Setter leaped from their
horses and tackled him. As Nantaje crashed to the ground,
he half wished there had been a white man's game that
would have prepared him for this sort of activity. Instead,
shackled at the wrists, he could do nothing but try to protect his head from their fists and his gut from their kicks.

"Someone go after her!" Butler ordered.

They worked Nantaje over hard until Butler broke it up.
Butler grabbed Nantaje's head by the hair and shoved the
barrel of his Colt into his face. "I ought to have them skin
you alive! I ought to kill the lot of you like I said I would!"

But Butler would not do that now. Nantaje had listened
to them making plans for all the money they were going to
get. They had come too far to throw away all their profits
because of one old lady.

Butler shoved him back to the ground. "I'd kill you now
except you're the only red devil here who can talk
English."

Nantaje sat up and dabbed the blood from his lip and a
gash in his forehead. Jakinda started for him. He stopped
her with a quick, guarded glance and she remembered.

There were sounds of horses and of men coming from
the darkness where they were beating the bushes for the
escaped woman. The noise faded for a moment as the
search widened; then hooves pounded back.

"She's gone. Scurried the hell out of here like a jackrabbit with a coyote on its tail," Green announced. "Probably

holed up in a crevice somewhere where we won't find her until daylight."

"We can't wait that long." Butler stalked back to his horse and gathered up its reins. "She'll be buzzard meat in a day or two anyway."

"Let's hope so," Green said dryly. He and Caulder had ridden back upon hearing the commotion.

"She's harmless, even if she somehow does manage to get back to civilization. Who's gonna listen to an old Apache squaw anyway?" Butler climbed into his saddle and glared dawn at Nantaje. "When this is over, buck, you and me, we're going to have us a serious talk." The sergeant ground his knuckles into his fist. "But for now I still need your jaw to work."

Nantaje stood painfully and brushed the dirt from his pants and shirt.

Butler started them moving again. Nantaje fell back in line, limping slightly now as he trudged along with the others.

They drove the people all night with no rest. In the morning, beneath a glaring sun, they finally came to a shrunken sink with bitter water. The men and horses drank first; then the Apache were allowed to drink, too, and fill their water skins.

Unlike the day before, there was no afternoon respite from the burning land. Butler let them rest half an hour, drink their fill, and chew what little food was left. Then they were moving again toward shimmering mountains growing tall and purple in the distance.

The sun slipped across the sky and evening came. They had reached the mountains now and were climbing a goat trail deep into them. The moon was larger tonight, the sky cloudless, and the air cold. Sometime later the people climbed a gravel embankment where iron rails snaked along the ground.

"The white man's railroad?" one of the other chained warriors asked softly. "Where does it go?"

Nantaje nodded toward the black mouth of a canyon ahead. "In there, I think."

They crossed a high trestle bridge above a narrow cut where far below moonlight danced upon the tumbling currents. Then the walls of the canyon closed in on either side. Tejon had nudged up close to Nantaje, but was careful not to show his true affection for his uncle. Jakinda remained near the rear of the column, where the women had formed their own group.

Deep darkness clung to the canyon floor where high, narrow walls kept the moonlight out. The prisoners marched on. After a while the defile widened; the walls fell away and a dark valley opened before them. Down there in the blackness came the flicker of distant lights.

"Montaña la Plata," one of the renegade soldiers said.

It was not a name Nantaje recognized, but then there were many places he did not know in this vast, rugged land. "Do you know of this village, Gato?" he asked the chief, who walked nearby.

"No."

Quiet inquiry revealed that none of them had ever heard of it. "It looks to be our destination," Nantaje remarked.

Gato merely nodded his head.

It was still dark, and they were much nearer when suddenly half a dozen riders burst from the shadows and surrounded them. Butler drew to a halt and waited for one of the men to ride a little closer.

"What is it you want, señor?"

"Come to see Francisco Ortega."

"Señor Ortega is not here." The Mexican studied Butler, then the Apache captives. "What is your business with the *patrón?*"

"My business is with Ortega, not with you."

"Your business will be with me first, señor, if you ever wish to speak to the *patrón*."

"Thought you said he wasn't here."

"Señor Francisco is not. But his brother, Señor Gaspar, he is."

"Ah! Gaspar. Yes, I can do business with him. All right, I'll tell you. See them 'paches? I brought them for Gaspar. Him, me, and the rest of his brothers, we made us a deal back in Nogales last year. Brought him a bunch of Injuns last spring. Reckon you weren't here or you'd remember me."

"I was here," the Mexican said with a frown. In the darkness his eyes gave back a bit more moonlight. "And I do remember now. Señor Butler, is it not?"

"That's right. Sam Butler."

The Mexican shrugged. "One gringo, he looks like another. I cannot always tell them apart."

The Mexican riders chuckled.

Butler stiffened, but said nothing. Nantaje knew that the smell of money was what dictated the sergeant's conduct.

"Señor Ortega is asleep still. You and your men come with me. I will take you somewhere to wait for the *patrón*."

"What about my Injuns?"

"My men will bring them to a holding place." He glanced over their numbers and nodded his head. "Señor Ortega will be pleased."

"Yeah, that's what I'm counting on. Only don't you go *counting* on these Injuns until we've gotten paid."

The Mexican turned his horse toward the scattered lights of the sleeping town, and Butler and his men left the Apache in the charge of Ortega's men.

The Mexicans marched the Indians alongside the looming bulk of a locomotive, toward a stockade of about a quarter acre, made of closely fitted rails. There were other stockades

51

about, all empty except for the next one over, which held about twenty or thirty people.

A dozen or so small fires burned near the corner posts, giving off enough light for Nantaje to see that most of those people were asleep. Yet a few stalked the perimeter like caged cats. He took note of the guard towers spaced evenly around the compound, making certain those stalking cats remained inside their cages.

His people were herded toward one of the empty pens. Rails were slid out of the way. Most of the people understood Spanish and followed the Mexicans' demands without complaint. Few would argue with the Winchesters and shotguns they used to wave them inside.

There was a fire pit in the middle of the compound filled with dry timber. One of the Mexicans carried a torch to it and set fire to the kindling. As the flames spread up through the cottonwood logs, the people gathered around for warmth.

When the Mexicans departed, Gato strode through his people, gathering his warriors around him. "We must make plans," he said quietly, considering each man there. Of all who had been in the village when the attack had come, only seven warriors had survived, and each of them was bound in iron and chains.

"What of these?" a man named Aluino asked. There was the soft clatter of chains as each man there inspected his shackles. "We must remove them," another said.

Gato said, "Words easily spoken, but how do we break the white man's chains?"

None there had an answer to that.

"Our problems are bigger than just shedding the white man's shackles," Nantaje said as he surveyed the dark land beyond the stockade and fires. "We have women and children to think about, too." The glare had dulled his night vision, but there seemed to be a dark ring of mountain peaks all around them. Whether they were solid or scattered ranges, he could not tell. The town was a dark row of buildings where perhaps a handful of lamps lent a bit of light. Not many people lived here now, but at one time there had been more.

Gato said, "We can slip into the night when the guards are not looking and make our way into those mountains and hide."

"Hide?" Nantaje scoffed. "For many years that is what we have done best. The guards will always be looking. There are six towers and two men in each. Those fires light the ground. All the ocotillo and mesquite have been cut back so that there is no cover."

"You would do nothing?" Gato asked, sarcasm edging the words.

"I did not say that." Nantaje considered a moment, his view lingering upon the next stockade over, where the people slept or quietly looked back at him. "Those people, do you not think they have planned to escape? But still they are here. If it was so easy as to wait until the guards were not looking, then they would not be here. No, I think escape is not so easy as that."

Another man spoke up. "Morning is not far off. When we see where we are, then we can make better plans. We cannot tell what is out there now."

They agreed that waiting for daylight was a wise idea. Nantaje pointed out that even if they did manage to somehow slip away, their absence would be immediately noticed. And without horses, they would be easily recaptured.

Gato said, "We will see what the morning brings; then we will talk more."

They were exhausted from their forced march. In a little while most of the women and children had curled up on the hard-packed ground and were asleep. Most of the men, too, but not Nantaje.

Nantaje was one of those cats that stalked the perimeter fencing, always wary, watching, thinking . . . planning.

* * *

". . . old times there are not forgotten, look away, look away, look away, Dixieland."

Louvel bent and pitched another chunk of twisted desert "driftwood" into the campfire.

"Oh, in Dixieland Ah'll take my stand to live or die in Dixie, look away, look away, look a—" Louvel stopped and glanced quickly to his left. His eyes probed the shadows, his ears suddenly tuned to the soft night sounds all around him. Something moved out there.

"Away, Dixieland." He reached into his bedroll for the old Spiller & Burr revolver hidden there, and ended his song. He listened, hearing only the crackle of his fire. There it was again. The scrape of iron against rock, and the even plodding of horses. Louvel buried the revolver beneath the blanket across his lap.

"Hello, the camp," a voice called from the darkness.

"Who are you?"

"Just some weary travelers," came the reply, carrying a heavy Mexican accent. "We see your fire, *amigo*. Think maybe we come and see who it is camped out here. Maybe Apache, we wonder."

"No Apache here, suh, Ah assure you. Come into the light where Ah can see you."

In a moment the darkness gave them up. Six Mexican riders ranged around him. Though heavily armed, none had a weapon drawn. For what purpose? Louvel mused. A lone one-armed man was no threat.

"Ah shot some blue quail earlier. You are welcome to what is left of them." He indicated the tin plate with the leftovers sitting near the fire. "It is still warm."

One of the men urged his horse a few steps closer and gave the sparse camp a quick look. His eyes lingered upon the rifle leaning against the bristling limbs of an ocotillo. Louvel noted the curious look that came to the Mexican's face.

"It's a Quackenbush safety rifle. Twenty-two caliber. Quite useless against men such as yourself, but quite effective against rabbits, grouse—and quail, especially the ones in this country, which seem to prefer to run along the ground than to take flight at the sight of danger. It is a single shot. No recoil. Just the thing for a one-armed man to use to fill his cookpot." Louvel lifted the stump of his right arm just in case they had not noticed.

"Quack . . . Quack-en-bousch?"

"Quackenbush. You may examine it if you wish."

The man stepped down off his horse and took up the rifle. He fiddled with the swiveling breech, sighted down the bore, then put the little rifle to his shoulder and squinted along its thin barrel.

"Quack-en-bousch!" He laughed and showed it around to his partners. Louvel let them have their joke. It was, after all, a funny little rifle from a Northern factory whose main contribution to mankind was nut crackers and nut picks. The man carefully set the rifle against the spiny branches of the tall cactus and everyone seemed more relaxed. Louvel relaxed, too, but his hand remained upon the blanket on his lap.

They dismounted and finished off what was left of the quail. Then they brought out a bottle of tequila and passed it around. Louvel took a pull from the bottle as it made the rounds.

"What is your name, señor?" the headman asked.

"Louvel. Royden Louvel of New Orleans, C.S.A."

"C.S.A.?" He laughed. No, señor, that country no longer exists."

"The Confederacy will always live, suh. If not as a place upon some map, then in the hearts of every freedom-loving man on this earth."

He laughed again and said, "I like you, señor."

"And who might you be, suh?"

"I am Santiago Ortega. This is my son Tomás, and my

other son, Porfirio." He pointed out two of the younger men, and then an older man. "My brother, Armando, and his three sons, Carlos, Ramiro, and Senon."

"A pleasure to meet you," Louvel said easily. A gambler never let his true feelings show, especially when he had just been introduced to four of the ten most-wanted men in the Arizona Territory.

"Tell me, Señor Louvel, what are you doing out here all alone, eh?" Santiago seemed to be sizing up his meager camp.

"Traveling, suh. Ah'm a man always on the move."

"Why?"

"Because Ah have no home anymore. The Yankees stole everything Ah once owned."

"But that was many years ago, no?"

"Many years? Ah wouldn't know. Time for me ceased to exist at three P.M. on April ninth, 1865."

Santiago looked at his friends as if not certain about Louvel's sanity. "So now where is it you are traveling to, Señor Louvel?"

Louvel shook himself as if coming out of a trance. "Ah thought Ah would try Santa Cruz."

"Santa Cruz? I know the place. Why there?"

Louvel smiled. "Because Ah hear the weather is pleasing, the señoritas are pretty, and the cardplaying is lively."

Santiago laughed. "*Sí!* It is all of that."

In the firelight Louvel saw that this Mexican had blue eyes. "And you, suh? Where might you and your family be heading at this late hour?"

Santiago's friendly smile dissolved, and a fiery hate erupted across his face. "We go to right a wrong. We go to find the killer of my sons, Diego, Pablo, Rodolfo. Murdered by the gringo named Keane."

Louvel looked up, surprised. Was that the same Keane who had saved his life in the streets of Tombstone only a couple of days earlier?

Santiago was suddenly suspicious. "Señor, do you know this *hombre?*"

"You say his name is Keane?" Louvel pretended to search his memory. "Ah have met so many men, it is hard to recall them all, Señor Ortega," he replied easily, disgusted with himself for the lapse that allowed a feeling to get past his carefully groomed, coolly unconcerned exterior. His hand drifted casually to the blanket as he leaned back against the cool sandstone boulder. "But Ah should not wish to be in his shoes right now."

Ortega was watching him.

Louvel feigned a yawn. "Where is it you go to look for this most unlucky man, suh?

"Porfirio, come here." Ortega waved for his son. "Tell me again where we can find this gringo who murdered your brothers."

The young man was taller than his father, but maybe thirty pounds lighter. He appeared nervous, and Louvel wondered if that was from fear of the man who had sired him. "He has a silver mine a couple of kilometers south of Tombstone, in the foothills of the Mule Pass Mountains. There is only one road and it is easy to find."

"That is where we go," Santiago said.

And Louvel was hoping they would go soon. He would have to sleep with one eye open if they decided to spend the night in his camp, and he did not want to do that. The farther away the notorious Ortega family was from him, the better he liked it. Santiago drew in a breath and let it out in a sudden gust. "I will not talk of this anymore."

"Ah am sorry my question brought on this torment. Ah know what it is like to lose family. The Second War of Independence took mine."

"*Sí.* Then we are much alike. We share the same pain of having our hearts wrenched from our breasts." He looked around Louvel's camp again, then frowned as if from some profound disappointment and turned away.

Louvel was glad he possessed nothing worth stealing.

Santiago said something in Spanish. Louvel didn't understand his words, but to his relief the men rose from the ground where they had been lounging and went to their horses. They moved wearily, as men did who had spent long hours in the saddle. Santiago turned back to Louvel.

"Thank you for the food, señor. We will go now. Tombstone is still a long ride."

"Good luck," Louvel said.

Santiago stepped up into his saddle and looked down at him. *"Vaya con Dios, señor."*

Santiago turned his animal away, then suddenly looked back at him and grinned. "See, you did not need the *pistola* under that blanket after all." He laughed and they rode off into the night.

Louvel didn't think he had been holding his breath, yet after they had left there was a long sigh in him, and when he had let go of it he felt drained and tired.

But he knew sleep would never come now. There was suddenly too much on his mind.

Chapter Five

The little coffee left in the bottom of his pot was still warm. Louvel poured it into his cup, grinds and all, and waited for them to settle. He could hear the quail talking to each other across the dark desert, and the other usual night sounds. He took comfort in that. It meant that he was alone again.

Louvel heaved a twisted piece of wood onto the fire and contemplated the cup in his hands. Santiago was out for Keane's blood, and he would probably get it, considering all the guns he had with him. What was John Keane to him anyway? Nothing. Just another Yankee in a land seemingly overrun with the vermin. And even if every lawman within two hundred miles had his eyes out for Santiago Ortega or one of his kin, what of it? They had treated him cordially, had demanded nothing, had taken nothing.

Louvel tasted his coffee. Anger stirred deep within him and he tried to put it out of mind but couldn't. The fact of the matter was, John Keane had saved his life. Louvel knew he had hesitated, that he would not have gotten to his pistol in time, no matter what he had said at the time. He'd have been a dead man if Keane had not stepped in to help a stranger.

"Honor!" he scoffed aloud. "The curse of breeding and training." He had come away from West Point with more than a splendid understanding of the art of waging war. He had come away with a sense of duty and a sense of honor, heightened by his upbringing as a Southern gentleman. "A curse and a bane!"

Louvel thought the matter over.

"So what does a man of honor do now?"

There was no grand voice to boom the answer from out of the darkness, only his conscience nudging him.

"Damn." Honor was what Louvel valued most these days, for unlike family, possessions, and country, a man's honor could never be taken from him; it could only be given away.

Louvel tossed the rest of the gritty coffee onto his fire and made ready to leave. There would be no sleeping tonight, not if he was to reach Keane before the Ortegas did.

"Why a Yankee, Lord? Why did he have to be a damned Yankee?"

Gaspar Ortega stepped from the old general store, which had been converted into his living quarters, and stood a moment, glancing up and down the street as he rolled himself a cigarette. Gaspar was the oldest of the four brothers, and since the death of their father, the head of their family of crime. At sixty-two, he appeared the picture of good health: his hair still black, his swarthy face nearly free of deep sun and wind creases. His weight hadn't changed in twenty years. He strode down the abandoned street of Montaña la Plata with the bearing of a much younger man. But all this was only for appearances. Inside, Gaspar Ortega was racked with pain—mostly in his chest, but of late it had begun to move downward to his bowels. He was losing blood, too, but no one else knew this. The cough, however, he could not hide. Over the last two months it had become more violent, more painful.

With two of his hired men at his side, Ortega angled toward the saloon and stepped through the gaping doorway. The door had disappeared years ago, as had most of the tables and all the whiskey and tequila. All that remained were three battered tables, an old, dusty bar, and a few bottles of whatever kind of rotgut the men who worked for Gaspar Ortega had brought with them.

Although no longer in any condition to be called a saloon, the building was still solid. It had been a convenient place for Sam Butler and his men to wait for the morning and the arrival of the *patrón* of this once thriving company town.

"Señor Butler. It is good to see you again."

Butler came across the dusty room and the men shook hands. Gaspar's shake was firm, and he managed a smile in spite of the pain he kept to himself.

"I am told you have brought me more merchandise?"

"Thirty-seven Apache. Mostly women and children, but a few strong bucks."

"I shall like to see them."

"They are in one of the holding pens," the man at Gaspar's side said. It was the same Mexican who had met Butler on the road the night before.

"And they'd better all still be there." Butler gave the Mexican a warning stare.

"I am sure they are," Gaspar said easily, smoothing the ruffled feathers. He looked at Butler's men, slumped upon the tabletops or against the walls. "Have you and your men eaten?"

"No, not yet, except for what little we had left."

"Leandro, see that these men get some food."

Leandro Menendez had been with Ortega almost two

61

years, and in that time he'd moved up through the ranks to become one of the *patrón*'s most trusted men. He stood five feet, eight inches tall, with the shoulders and arms of a fighter, but with the lean legs of a dispatch runner. He might have been in his late thirties, but he never spoke of himself or his past. A taciturn man who rarely smiled, Leandro Menendez seemed to be haunted by ghosts from his past. He was a man of deep feelings, and always wary of them, as if afraid that if he dropped his guard for an instant those hidden secrets would somehow take over the reins of his life.

"*Sí, patrón,*" Leandro said, hurrying off.

Gaspar coughed briefly into his shirtsleeve, then cleared his throat. "While Leandro is arranging breakfast for you and your men, let's go look at what you have brought me, eh?"

They started for the edge of town. Gaspar flicked the stub of his cigarette away and rolled another, offering the paper and tobacco to Butler, who fixed himself a smoke, too. The men leaned upon the rails of the pen, looking at the Apache.

"You are right, señor, many women and children."

"Some of the warriors were off making trouble. Rumor has it they joined up with Geronimo." Butler frowned, then filled his lungs with smoke. "Some we had to shoot. Couldn't be helped."

"Too bad." Gaspar shook his head.

"What are you paying now for women and children?"

Gaspar thought it over. "I can give seven dollars in silver for each of them."

"Seven? It was ten last spring."

The Mexican shrugged. "The mines, they have cut back what they pay me."

"Like hell."

Gaspar gave a small smile. "You can always take them back with you."

"Take them back? And do what with them?" Butler glared at the huddled Indians. His scowl fell upon Nantaje and deepened before shifting back to Gaspar. "All right. Seven for women and children. What about the bucks? Bucks had better be worth a hell of a lot more."

"Eighteen in silver for each."

"You're a thief."

Gaspar grinned.

"Make it twenty. You're already cutting my throat with the women and children."

The Mexican considered, then turned toward the captives, picking out each man with his finger as his lips wordlessly counted them. "All right, my friend. Twenty each for the men."

Butler nodded. "You are an old pirate. As usual, you have stolen them from me, Señor Ortega. You got yourself a deal."

Ortega laughed and they shook on the agreement. "A pleasure to do business with you again, Señor Butler." A sudden, racking cough ended the deal. Then it passed and Gaspar Ortega pulled himself erect and dragged his sleeve across his mouth.

Butler said, "That don't sound too good."

"An annoyance, is all. It will go away soon." The men walked back into town.

A food wagon arrived about midday. "Come and get it while you can," a stout Mexican announced in Spanish and began ladling gruel into tin bowls and passing them through the rails.

Nantaje moved into line with the others. Tejon and Jakinda were just ahead of him. Neither he nor Jakinda acknowledged the other, although they exchanged glances. He wished he could encourage her, but there seemed little to be encouraged about. The Mexican handed him a bowl with a wooden spoon, and Nantaje took it off by himself to eat. It was a tasteless blend of boiled wheat and oats, but the people were hungry and no one complained.

Gato and another warrior joined him. "There are guards everywhere," Gato said, glancing around the compound. He nodded at the next pen over, separated from theirs by fifty feet of open ground. The food wagon had progressed to it, and the fat cook was passing out bowls of the same bland fare. "I wonder how many days they have been here."

The other man said, "There were some words passed before the guards came by last night. They have been here for two weeks. No one knows why. But that was all that could be said before we were told to quit talking."

Nantaje sniffed the air, heavy with the odor of human feces. "I could have told you that without asking."

Gato squinted up at the brassy sky. "With no place to hide from the sun, I am surprised many have not died."

"Many have," Nantaje said. He had spent the morning carefully surveying their prison and the town that lay only a few hundred feet beyond. What was particularly curious was the locomotive with its string of cattle cars that sat idle on a siding just beyond the corrals. But it was what he had discovered by observing the comings and goings of the Mexicans, and the work they were doing some distance away, that he was speaking of now. "Over there, beyond that ridge, I have seen men with shovels. Twice now a wagon has gone out to them and bodies were unloaded."

The third man frowned. "The children will die first, then the older men and women. Why do they hold us here? To see how long we can live on boiled grain and bad water?"

Gato shook his head. "Even if we could get these chains off our wrists, we could not get the women and children to safety; not on foot, with no weapons, not even a knife."

Nantaje agreed. "It is impossible for everyone to leave, but one man might make it out and bring back many warriors."

"Many warriors?" Gato scoffed. "There are no more

warriors. The few still free are with Geronimo, and he is in hiding. No one will come for us. If we are to escape, it must be by our own cunning."

"I was not thinking of Apache warriors, Gato."

"Then who?"

"The cavalry."

They looked at Nantaje as if perhaps the sun had already boiled his brains.

"It is so. If I can slip free of here and steal a horse, I could ride to Fort Bowie. I know many soldiers there. I would speak to Captain McGowan and he would send soldiers to arrest these renegades, and to free our people."

"You think the white chief would do that?" Gato asked.

"Many of our people have ridden with the white soldiers. We have helped them find the Chiricahuas and Mimbres, have showed them the secret ways into their hidden camps. The white man would not have been able to put even one of Geronimo's or Nana's people on the reservation if not for our people."

"And they would honor that?"

"Yes. They would."

Gato thought this over, then lifted his hands and snapped the chain that connected the iron cuffs. "And what of these?"

Nantaje grinned. "I have learned much by living with the white man. I keep my mouth closed and my ears open, and my eyes take in everything, like the white soldiers' sponges that take up water until the bowl is empty. I have played cards and dominoes with those who watch the stockades. Those men understand much of these chains, and how they are fashioned, and how they can be opened . . . even without a key. Sometimes they make a game of it, marking their time by a clock. Once when I asked about the game, one man showed me how it was done."

"How what was done?"

Now Nantaje snapped the chain. "Tonight, when it is

late and the fires have burned low, I will shed these as the snake sheds his skin."

Gato frowned. "If you can do this, then remove the chains from all of us."

"No. They would notice that at once. They would become suspicious if even two or three of us are missing. But one warrior just might slip away unnoticed."

Evening cooled the sweltering land, bringing some small amount of comfort to the suffering Apache. With the setting of the sun the food wagon returned as if it, like so many of the creatures of the desert, had hidden away during the heat of the day, too, only to venture out again once the sun had sunk below the ragged mountain peaks to the west. The people knew the routine by now and lined up for their bowl of food from the black cauldron.

This time, Butler and three of his soldiers were there with them, looking over the dark faces taking the food. Nantaje joined the others in line for food, but when his turn came, Butler motioned him over and stepped down to the corner of the stockade as if he wanted to speak to him privately. Nantaje went over, keeping back from the rails, out of Butler's reach. His men stayed close to their boss.

"What is it you want?" Nantaje asked.

"Just wanted to thank you for translating my words to your people. I know you didn't want to do it, and we was kinda hard on you, but you gotta understand, it was business, that's all. I ain't got nothing against you or your people personally."

"And that is what you want to tell me now?" Nantaje doubted the man's every word, and kept back a safe distance.

"I know you don't trust me, and I can't say as I blame you. I just wanted to let you know how we really feel. Oh, and that thing with the old lady the other night? I'm happy she got off like she done. I didn't really want to kill her

66

anyway. I was mad, you see. Said some things I didn't really mean." He looked at the people packed like cattle in the corrals. "You and your people will only be here a few more days. Then Ortega will put you on that train over there for a trip to the Gulf of California, where there will be a steamer waiting to take you into Guadalajara. Things will be better for you down there."

"Guadalajara?" Nantaje had heard of the city far south of the United States' border, but knew nothing of it. "Why are we to be taken there?"

"There's work for your people to do," Butler said. "Well, I just wanted to let you know. We both served together at one time, remember? There's a certain bond between men who serve in the same outfit." Butler stuck a hand through the rail.

Nantaje would have rather taken a serpent's mouth into his fist.

"Can't say as I blame you." He turned to leave, then seemed to remember something. "What are they feeding you here?"

Nantaje showed him the bowl.

Butler's mouth screwed up in disgust. "Pretty rank fare." He reached under the dirty blue uniform blouse and came out with a loaf of dark bread. "Gaspar Ortega sets a grand table. I took this from it at dinner. Here. It will make that slop go down a mite easier."

Nantaje hesitated, but the bread tempted him. He was not thinking so much of himself as his sister and nephew. It would help them stay strong, especially if what Butler had said was true, that they were bound for a long trip. Nantaje did not intend to be on that train when it left, and if he moved fast, neither would his people. He hated taking a handout from this man, but his people were hungry and the little food they were given was deplorable.

"Go on, take it," Butler urged.

Nantaje stepped closer, his eyes wary and riveted upon

the man holding the bread out to him. There seemed to be little danger. All Butler's hand held was the bread, and Nantaje could take it before the sergeant could grab him. Nantaje made a quick stab for it.

Out the corner of his eye he saw something move. Instantly he realized his mistake. One of Butler's men had been standing to one side looking bored with the meeting. Now suddenly he came to life and shot an arm through the rails, grabbing the chain between Nantaje's wrists. He gave a sharp yank. The bowl of gruel went flying and his chin bashed into the rails. The other soldiers immediately pounced on him, dragging his arms through until they had him hitched up tight against the wood.

Butler's friendly face hardened. "I told you I'd get you, you red son of a bitch!" he said in a growl, shoving his face so close Nantaje could smell the sweat and tobacco and whiskey. Butler dropped the bread and ground it into the sand with the heel of his boot. Then his fist bunched and shot through the rails, driving deep into the Apache's gut.

Breath exploded from Nantaje. He struggled to free himself but they pulled him even tighter against the rails. Another blow crashed into his jaw. Blinding light burst before his eyes as Butler tore into him. Nantaje felt consciousness slipping away. Some of his people rushed to help, but Butler's men drew their guns. All the Apache could do was stand there and watch.

Suddenly there was a commotion outside the rails. Nantaje was too far gone to know what it meant, but all at once the soldiers released him and he slumped to the ground. His ears were buzzing like a thousand hornets, yet through it he heard a man coughing, then his voice firming up and barking angrily.

"These people are no longer in your charge, Señor Butler. What is the meaning of this?"

"That buck caused me trouble on the way and I promised he'd pay for it."

"He is no longer your concern. If I was not a generous man, I would have my men kill you right now. He is valuable property and you may have lowered his value to my buyers! Orlando, Miguel, get these men out of here."

At the rattle of rifles Nantaje struggled to open an eye that was swiftly swelling shut. Butler and his men were being escorted away.

Gaspar Ortega remained there, peering down at him through the rails. "Leandro, you and Hernando see to his injuries. We don't want our investments dying on us between here and Guadalajara."

They slid the rails aside and two men grabbed Nantaje by the arms and dragged him out of the corral, across the railroad tracks, and into a nearby building.

The wet cloth they used to clean the gashes on his face revitalized him. His jaw ached but was not broken. There was pain deep inside him, below his ribs, that eased a bit when they gave him a little cool water to drink.

One of the Mexicans said, "That man, you make him very angry, yes?"

"He would have killed an old woman. I stopped him." It hurt to speak.

Shadows filled the building where they had taken him, and one of the guards was busy lighting lanterns. Nantaje saw more of the place as the light improved. It looked a little like the barracks back at Fort Bowie. A dozen or so cots stood in lines along the walls, and in the center of the floor was a round rifle rack with five or six rifles in it, about the same number as there were sleeping men. There was a trapdoor in the ceiling with a ladder leading up through it. Nantaje's view halted and his eyes narrowed. Just visible up there was a carriage wheel, and the distinctive bronze jacket that surrounded the barrels of a Gatling gun.

"Are you expecting trouble?" Nantaje asked.

One of the Mexicans laughed. "We keep waiting for trouble, but it never comes. No one is *loco* enough to try and take Gaspar Ortega's silver away from him. Montaña la Plata is a dead man's grave for anyone who might try."

"Gaspar Ortega? Is he the one who ordered Butler off of me?"

"Yes, that is Señor Ortega. Him and his three brothers, they run this place."

"Three? They are here?"

"They are away, but they come often."

"And they have silver here?"

"Enough to fill that wagon," the Mexican announced, pointing out the window at a freight wagon parked alongside the building.

"No more of this, Hernando," Leandro said, giving the first a warning look. "You talk too freely. This one seems not to be badly hurt. Let's return him to the corral with the others."

They helped Nantaje to his feet then and escorted him back outside. Between two buildings, tucked back in the shadows, Nantaje spied an artillery piece and a caisson of ammunition. The place was indeed like Fort Bowie, in more ways than one. He wondered just how many men—and how much in the way of armaments—the Ortegas commanded here.

Back in the corral, his sister went to him. They didn't speak, but relief filled her face when she saw that in spite of his blackened and swollen face, he still managed a smile for her. She held Tejon back as the men went off to talk.

Nantaje told Gato and the others what he had learned, and that he would make his break tonight. Tomorrow might be too late if Ortega was planning to ship his people down to Guadalajara in the next few days.

Chapter Six

When Nantaje laid out his plan, everyone agreed one man might slip away unseen, though some were reluctant that it should be Nantaje. But Nantaje spoke the white man's language, and he knew the soldiers at Fort Bowie. There was no other choice.

Shortly after nightfall, the Mexicans built up the perimeter fires. If it was the same tonight as the previous night, around three or four in the morning the guards would become careless, and the fires would burn low. The hours drifted past. Shortly after midnight Nantaje rose from his place near the dying fire. His silent footsteps gave no warning. Jakinda whirled around, startled to discover him there. He hunkered down beside her, his voice low so as not to wake the sleeping people scattered around the enclosure.

"Soon it will be time."

"Can you do it?"

"I can, but I need your help."

"Me?"

"Gato and the others know the plan. Before I disappear, there must be a diversion. There will be a quarrel between Gato and Aluino. It will wake the people. I need you to tell them to stand behind the fire over there. Gato will have built up the blaze so that it will cast your shadows across the ground, to the rails, over there." He inclined his head to a spot where two men seemed to be asleep. They weren't really asleep, but Jakinda did not need to know every detail of their plans.

"You can begin passing the word to those who sleep nearby, and they can pass it on."

Jakinda nodded. "I will." She glanced at the chains. "I hear that a snake will shed his skins tonight."

He grinned. "For that, I will need your help, too."

"How can I help free you of those chains?"

"I need a pin from your hair."

Giving him a questioning look, Jakinda reached back and withdrew one of the long wooden pins that held her hair in place. She had shaped it from mesquite, and it was hard and strong.

He inserted the pin into the keyhole and began moving it around.

"What are you doing?"

"Inside this hole are little pegs. Each peg must line up with the other. It is the secret of the lock that was taught to me by white jailers at Fort Bowie. What I must do is line them up. It can be done by feel only, yet some men become very good at it. When they leave the army, they make much money by what they have learned. The whites call it 'picking the lock.' I have not done it for a long time."

"But you remember how?"

There was a small metallic click and the first cuff fell away. "I remember how." The second cuff took a while longer to puzzle out, but soon it, too, gave up the secret of the little pegs. Nantaje grinned as he returned the cuffs to his wrists but left them unlatched. "Start passing the word."

"Be careful, my brother."

"Be strong, my sister. I will be back for you and Tejon and the others." Nantaje crept through the sleeping bodies, and at the campfire joined the few men who had remained awake. "I am ready." He showed Gato the open cuffs. "Jakinda will make sure the people hide the firelight while you and Aluino distract the guards."

Gato nodded and began tossing wood into the fire. "We will do our part; you do yours." Gato built up the flames. Nantaje went to the railings, where a few men slept. He curled up on the ground as if going to sleep himself . . . and waited.

Gato had the fire blazing; its flames leaped and its light danced across the compound and the sleeping bodies there. It was bright enough to kill the night vision of any guard who happened to look at it. Nantaje was careful to keep his eyes averted, focused upon the dark locomotive that sat upon the nearby tracks.

He used his ears instead of his eyes to follow what was happening. Suddenly Gato snapped some words out, and Aluino growled an oath. It had begun. The people began to stir, and Nantaje prepared to move. The sound of scuffling reached his ears, and as it grew, the bright firelight dimmed across the ground where he was lying. Jakinda had done her part. Drawn by the harsh words, the people had begun to gather in front of the fire, their bodies casting long shadows across the compound.

"Are you ready?" one of the men who had pretended to be asleep asked.

"I am."

The other said, "The hole is tight, but you can squeeze through. Move quickly so we might cover you."

"Look for me. What is happening?"

The first replied, "The guards are watching Gato and Aluino, as we hoped."

"Good. Let's do it now."

The two men rose from the ground and stood there, staring toward the quarreling men. Behind them, Nantaje rolled to the fence, where the lower railing nearly brushed the ground. But beneath it a small hollow had been excavated. He slipped into it, his chest scraping the bottom of the rail, and he was outside the compound. Trusting that the distraction had drawn the guards' attention, and that the brightness of the campfire had dulled their eyes, Nantaje hunched low and dashed for the locomotive. He threw himself to the ground, rolled under it, and scurried behind the huge iron wheels.

Once he had slipped from the compound, Gato and Aluino finished their argument and the people drifted off again to their blankets.

For a long while Nantaje did not move but lay there listening, waiting for an alarm. None sounded. He had escaped undetected and started forward between the rails, taking care not to run into any of the iron machinery just inches above his head. From beneath the cow catcher he surveyed the town. Few lights lit the place, and for the moment all was quiet. He knew there was a corral at the far end where he could take a horse.

Nantaje pulled himself from under the locomotive and sprinted to the corner of a nearby building, then worked his way through the weeds growing up behind them. At one of the side streets he stopped and crept along it to examine the artillery piece he'd spied earlier. It was a cannon, a twelve-pounder, with a caisson of powder and explosive shells.

He heard voices and dropped to the ground and scurried beneath the caisson. Up the street two Mexicans emerged from a building where the pale glow of lantern light washed dimly across the road. They strolled past the caisson then turned down another street. Nantaje gave them another minute, then sprang to his feet and hurried through the shadows toward the corrals.

Then a man stepped around a dark corner and blocked his way. It was the one called Leandro. Nantaje recognized him at once and drew up, casting about for some avenue of escape. But instead of sounding an alarm, Leandro just stood there considering him. He was carrying a rifle, but made no effort to use it. Then all at once he turned from him and moved casually away. Nantaje was dumbfounded, and he didn't have time to ponder it, yet as he started off again, he was certain he heard Leandro whisper, "Go with God, my son."

The old livery stable appeared unused, but when he got closer he smelled burning coal oil and spied the faint outline of light from around a door. He pressed an ear to it. Muffled voices came from beyond. Around the side of the building he sidled up to a dingy window and peeked inside. Three men were sitting at a table playing cards and carrying on a friendly conversation. Nearby was another Gatling gun and two crates of ammunition. Nantaje grinned. The Ortega brothers were well prepared to keep their silver . . . and anything else of value they might have in this ghost town.

He climbed quietly into the corral, making soft, calming sounds as he moved among the horses. His army mount was there, but he wanted an Apache horse for this trip; one of those short, stout animals that had run wild across the south-western deserts since the days of the Spanish conquistadors. He picked a mare he thought would have a level head and good legs; he led her to the gate and slid back the rails.

"Hey, you!" A man appeared in a lighted doorway. "Who is that out there?" he demanded, peering hard into the night.

"Hernando," Nantaje called back, remembering the name of the other guard who had tended his wounds.

"Hernando?" he roared.

"What do you want?" asked a voice from inside.

"It seems you can be in two places!" the first man shouted. "We got a runaway!" He reached back inside and came around with a rifle.

Nantaje didn't wait to see what would happen next. Grabbing a fistful of mane, he swung onto the mare's back. A shot rang out. He drove his heels into her flank, and she gave a startled leap. He pointed her nose up the main street and lay low along her neck as the dark building swept past. More gunshots shattered the night. Then he was past the locomotive and the last building, and pounding along the road that led to the narrow place where the tracks came through the hills.

The staccato bark of the Gatling gun ripped the night. Nantaje held tight as the horse flew down the road. Finally the blasts ceased and the only sounds he heard were the pounding of the horse's hooves and her heavy breathing as she raced on, her sides heaving and her heart thumping beneath his thighs. They would be coming after him. Soon. For now, he put that out of his mind and concentrated on his riding, on the hills looming ahead, and what he would do once beyond the canyon entrance and out in the desert. The desert was the Apache's natural environment, and once there he could easily elude his pursuers.

He glanced over his shoulder. The town seemed far behind him now, too far to tell if Ortega's men had yet mounted their pursuit.

Nantaje turned back to the dark, rugged mountain looming before him and leaned low into the rushing wind. Luck was with him so far . . . if it would only hold out until he reached Fort Bowie.

Hiding amid the shadows, Nantaje watched as a company of Ortega's men emerged from the mouth of the canyon. There were eight of them, and they drew rein and attempted to search for his tracks in the feeble light of the coming dawn. But they didn't search very long or very hard. As if understanding the hopelessness of tracking an Apache in this country, the men merely went through the motions until enough time had passed that they could claim to have put an honest effort into the chase. Finally they turned back empty-handed to report his escape to Gaspar Ortega.

Nantaje quietly left the area, urging his horse ahead, pointing her toward the Mexican border and Fort Bowie. Daylight brightened the rugged umber countryside, showing a wild, beautiful, and unfamiliar landscape. Desert mountains rose in front of him and behind, rocky and barren, scattered with ocotillo and mesquite and a few stately saguaros with arms reaching for the sky like old men praying to the sun.

Nantaje pushed on, and the mare ran her heart out for him. Though it was still early, the air was already hot. Nantaje slowed her as they climbed a rocky bluff, where he dismounted to survey this part of the Sonoran desert. He recognized none of it, but intuitively he knew the way to go. He peered back the way he had come, at the mountains that were but a distant haze of saw teeth upon the desert floor, and ahead, at the hot, barren hills that he was about to cross.

He needed to find water. Leading the animal down into a swale, Nantaje followed a trace of green that would have gone unnoticed by most men. He studied the lay of the rocks, even those uplifts miles away that appeared meaningless. But to the Apache they were a road sign pointing to water, and it didn't take long before he flushed a covey of quail. Searching among the rocky hillside, he found the plants he was looking for. The seep wasn't much more than a glistening streak of moisture upon the sandstone. Carefully removing a few rocks, Nantaje excavated a shallow bowl that slowly filled with water. A few minutes of waiting produced enough water to quench his thirst. He let the precious moisture accumulate again so the horse could have her share, too.

Then he was moving again. He pressed on throughout the heat of the day, and with the coming of evening had reached familiar land. Turning due north, he pushed hard into the gathering night. The horse never faltered. A wild descendent of the famous Spanish barb, she responded to Nantaje's demands as if she had been bred for this kind of punishment. Early the next morning Nantaje passed the abandoned Butterfield stage station.

He dismounted to water the exhausted horse at the wooden trough at Apache Pass, where a rusty iron pipe tapped into the ancient spring there.

Fort Bowie was just ahead.

Captain McGowan listened without interrupting, nodding his head in silent agreement with many parts of Nantaje's story. Nantaje ended by saying, "My people will be taken far away, to Guadalajara, if help does not arrive."

McGowan leaned back in the chair, the morning sunlight through the adjutant's office window striking his prematurely white hair, his gray eyes thoughtfully considering the ex-scout as he deliberated.

"Butler, you say?" McGowan leafed through some papers upon his desk and found what he was looking for. He glanced at the long list of names. "Here he is." McGowan handed the paper across, but Nantaje had only the vaguest understanding of the white man's written words. "You can see the list of deserters is quite long. Sixty-two on that page, and that is just from the companies here at Fort Bowie and Fort Huachuca. Although the army would like to catch them and haul each and every one of them back to face a court-martial, I just don't have the men to do it right now. With Geronimo on the one hand, and the five thousand Apache at San Carlos on the other, we have our men stretched thin, even with the new recruits

Sheridan has been sending." McGowan shook his head, the regret in his voice sincere. "I'm sorry, Nantaje, but I can't afford a detachment to run down a handful of deserters hiding in Mexico."

"But my people need your help. We have always been at peace with the whites. We have scouted for you, have fought the Mimbres and Chiricahuas for you. Now that we need your help, you can refuse us?"

"Look, it's not just the lack of men," he went on. "General Miles has put Lieutenant Gatewood and twenty-five troops across the border to watch the flanks of the Sierra Madre, trying to run down Geronimo. We can't keep sending men into Mexico without risking an incident. The government turns its head when some of our patrols happen to cross over, but how long can we expect Mexican authorities to keep looking the other way?"

Nantaje stood there, stunned. The army had been his only hope, and now he understood how misplaced that hope had been.

McGowan said, "Listen, I know this is urgent, and I'd like to help, but a decision to send a patrol into Mexico to rescue a band of Apache will have to come from above me. General Miles is using Fort Huachuca as his advanced headquarters and forward supply depot for the Geronimo campaign. I'll send a dispatch down to him and tell him of the matter. We'll have to wait for his reply."

"There is no time to wait, Captain McGowan. The Ortegas will move my people in a couple of days. Once they do, there will be no way to get them back. They will die as slaves digging for the silver in the ground. What must be done must be done now. I cannot wait for the general to make up his mind."

"What will you do?"

Nantaje shook his head. "I don't know. But I will have to think of something."

McGowan frowned, then nodded. "I understand completely. I wish I could help, but as I said, my hands are tied."

Rage burned hot within Nantaje's breast, but he kept it inside as he left McGowan sitting behind his desk. Outside, he strode angrily toward his horse, not even noticing that his old friend Bud Wilson had been standing there, waiting for him.

"I take it the captain said no," Wilson said, catching up to the scout.

"It might cause an *incident!*" Nantaje shot back. He turned suddenly, fierce black eyes boring into the lieutenant. "As if his renegade soldiers taking my people is not already an incident! He would wait for word from the white chief, Miles, before sending soldiers to help my people. He tells me he can do nothing. His hands are tied." Nantaje spat out the words angrily.

"I'm sorry, Nantaje. If it weren't for this uniform, I'd ride with you. You know that, don't you?"

"I believe you would, but if you came with me now you would be a deserter. Your name would be number sixty-three on Captain McGowan's list."

"Huh?"

"Your army has much trouble keeping their soldiers in camp. Many wander."

Wilson gave a short laugh. "Well, considering the poor pay, horrible working conditions, and harsh punishments for even the smallest infractions, you can hardly blame them."

Nantaje gathered up the horse's mane in his fist.

"Your animal looks all done in. She can use some rest. Come with me and I'll tell the sergeant in charge of the stables to give her a bucket of oats."

"No time. I've got to get back to my people. I can't let Ortega send them away to die in the silver mines."

Wilson grabbed Nantaje's arm. "By yourself? From what you told me, his place is a fortress."

"I have no other choice."

"Damn!" Wilson growled. "You'd think McGowan could make this decision on his own!"

"If Butler had taken whites instead of Apache, he would send soldiers."

"Unfortunately, you're right. And that don't make me feel any better about it, Nantaje."

"There are few whites who care what happens to the Apache. Most want us on the reservation, and many would see us in the grave."

Nantaje swung up onto the horse and settled wearily upon her back. He needed rest, too, but there was no chance of that just yet.

Wilson's forehead wrinkled under the blazing sun. "You can't do it alone, Nantaje."

"There is no one else."

"Perhaps there is one."

Nantaje saw that Wilson had a thought he was working through. "Who?"

"You're right; there are few whites who care much what happens to the Apache, but I just remembered one who would. In fact, he lost his command because he tried."

Nantaje wore a puzzled look; then his dark eyes brightened. "Yes, I remember the one you speak of."

Wilson nodded. "Major J. R. Keane."

"Yes, John Russell Keane." Nantaje thought a moment. "But he quit the army many years ago."

"Quit?" Wilson shook his head. "He didn't quit. Major Keane was forced out. At least General Crook was decent enough to give him the choice. It was either resign and keep his pension, or face a court-martial."

"But would he help?"

"I don't know. It's worth a chance."

Nantaje nodded. "Perhaps he might, but John Russell Keane is not here."

"No, he isn't, but I've got a couple buddies at Fort

Huachuca who say they see him from time to time over in Tombstone. The army has established a heliograph station in the Mule Pass Mountains. I heard one of the heliographers assigned to it saying Major Keane was digging for silver thereabouts. You have to go right past those mountains on your way down into Mexico. I'd ask a few questions once I got there."

"Even if he did help, that would make only two of us," Nantaje pointed out, not encouraged.

"You can look at it that way, or you might say that if he does join your cause, you've increased your strength a hundred percent."

Nantaje peered at Wilson, momentarily mystified; then he laughed. "With that logic, it is no wonder the army has not captured Geronimo and his handful of braves."

Wilson grinned and extended a hand. "Good luck." Nantaje took it. Wilson stepped back from the horse. "If you find Major Keane, tell him Bud Wilson is still around . . . and that he's still a lowly lieutenant in this man's army."

"I will tell him."

"Nantaje."

"Yes?"

"You take care of yourself, and you take care of those people of yours."

Nantaje turned the horse away and kicked her into motion, wondering if he could even find John Russell Keane after all these years.

And if he did, would Keane be willing to help him get his people back?

Chapter Seven

Royden Louvel had ridden hard all night, but if the Ortegas had not stopped somewhere along the way to rest, they were still ahead of him, and he doubted he could find Keane in time to give him a warning. But honor dictated that he at least try. He met a man along the road leading a mule packed heavy with the trappings of a miner. The man knew of Keane, knew where he'd staked his claim, and liked to talk. He happily gave the one-armed Southerner directions on how to get there in exchange for the news that Santiago and his boys were in the area.

He found the trail that led off the main road into the desert mountains. His horse picked its way along the hot, rocky ground until the terrain dipped into a cool, forested valley. A couple of hundred yards beyond, sitting on a bluff near a pile of stones, Louvel spied the cabin, weathered and leaning a bit to one side.

He clucked his horse forward, stopping again a few dozen feet from the cabin.

"Keane! Are you in there?" Beyond he could see a horse and a mule, and both appeared packed and ready to go.

"Major Keane, can you hear me, suh?" he called.

Stones clattered behind him. He turned. Keane was standing there, a rifle resting easily in the crook of his arm, his hat low over his eyes, and a six-gun at his hip.

"Well, if it isn't Capt. Royden Louvel—of the New Orleans Louvels. To what do I owe the honor of your visit?"

"You've said it, suh. To honor, and nothing else, Ah assure you."

"Honor, eh?" Keane came closer and gave a short laugh. "Get down off that horse, Captain, and come inside. I was just about to leave this good-for-nothing hunk of real estate, but there is a barrel of water inside and a little food left over. You look like you can use both."

Louvel dismounted and walked his horse alongside the big man. Keane had the wide shoulders and brawny arms of a common laborer, but his eyes were those of a philosopher. They seemed to look through a man to his very soul. And there was a hint of a smile, as if the man was constantly guarding it. Louvel had the feeling that Keane would always understand more than he would let on.

"You may not wish to tarry, suh."

"Oh? And why might that be?"

"Because there is a man named Santiago Ortega who even now is on his way with several men, family members of his. Apparently you killed three of his sons."

"I did indeed."

"Santiago intends to have his revenge."

They went inside and Louvel peered curiously at the bullet holes. Keane grinned and said, "Those are compliments of the Ortega brothers. They were intended for me."

Louvel nodded and took a tin cup from Keane. The water cut the dust from his mouth and eased his dry throat.

"Have some bread. It's gone hard, but no mold yet. I was just going to leave it for the coyotes and bears."

"Why are you leaving?"

"Why, Captain Louvel? Because I've spent two years of my life looking for something that wasn't here."

Louvel considered him a moment. "Why do Ah get the feeling you are not referring to gold or silver?"

"Because you are a man of perception. Must be all that West Point training."

"You did not attend West Point?"

"Never had the opportunity. I worked my way up through the ranks from a private." Keane grinned. "Of course, the war helped out. Battlefield commissions are about the only way to earn rank in the army anymore."

"That speaks much for your abilities, suh."

"As a soldier, yes. It doesn't help much in mining silver. No aptitude at all in that endeavor."

"Then why did you retire? You are still a young man." Louvel saw immediately that he had opened an old wound. "Ah'm sorry, suh. Ah see Ah am prying where Ah am not wanted. It seems to be a bad habit of mine."

"Better finish packing." Keane grabbed up his saddlebags and went outside and lashed them to the back of his saddle. When he came back the hint of a smile returned. "Thanks for bringing me the warning. I know it wasn't easy."

"Honor, suh—"

"Is everything?" Keane completed.

"Indeed."

"Then you and I agree on that, at least. And that is why I left the army." Back outside he shoved his rifle into its saddle boot and swung up onto his horse, settling himself comfortably upon the saddle. "I know a way out of here that avoids that trail you came by. I'd just as soon not run into the Ortegas, if I can help it."

"Ah will ride with you to the road," Louvel said, mounting up.

"I will welcome the company, Captain." Keane looked around the claim, and his gaze lingered a moment upon the hole gouged out of the tough ground, then upon the cabin. The worn-out structure appeared to be just waiting for him to leave so it could collapse upon itself. He peered long and hard across the high desert landscape, and finally gave a small nod, as if he approved of his decision to leave. Clucking softly, Keane got his animal moving and started down the rocky trail.

A rifle barked and a puff of white smoke billowed from a rise behind the cabin. The angry whine of a bullet buzzed past them, and Keane and Louvel dove from their saddles, Keane scrambling for the ground while Louvel yanked the Quackenbush from out of his bedroll.

Suddenly rifle fire erupted all along the ridge.

The two men tumbled down a slope and drew up under a small overhang of rock.

"I left my rifle up there," Keane said, scanning the high ground. The horses had taken off, and he watched his Winchester disappear with them.

"Ah have one."

"What the hell is that?"

"Quackenbush safety rifle," Louvel replied, working the breech and inserting a tiny rimfire cartridge.

"Can you hit anything with it?"

"Certainly, suh. But Ah won't guarantee Ah will stop it."

"Great." Keane peeked over the embankment. A rock shattered near his head, driving him back. "How many were there?"

"Seven, unless they picked up some more men along the way. They hold the high ground . . . there, and over there." He pointed with the .22 barrel.

"We are outflanked and outgunned."

"Just like the old days," Louvel commented beneath his breath, but loud enough for Keane to hear.

Keane thumbed a sixth cartridge into his Colt and snapped the loading gate shut. "How fast can you load that thing?"

"Faster than Ah can load my revolver, Ah assure you." Louvel touched the old cap-and-ball percussion piece in the flap holster on his belt, then pointed at a low stretch of ground. "If you go that way, and Ah to the left, we will be able to put some distance between ourselves and set up a crossfire."

"A tactician?"

"West Point had its benefits."

Keane grinned. "You head for those mesquite up there. Try to keep their heads down with that pip-squeak rifle of yours while I work my way around back of them."

Santiago's men poured in the lead when they moved out.

Louvel crawled up behind the mesquite and put the rifle down. He fished a box of cartridges out of his pocket, placing it conveniently at hand, then shouldered the Quackenbush, rested its barrel on the stump of his right arm, and fired at the spot where he'd first seen the gunsmoke. The puny crack of the .22 was not a thing to inspire confidence. Undaunted, Louvel swiveled open the breech and reloaded. Being outnumbered and outgunned was not new to the ex-Confederate officer. He fired again, keeping one eye on Keane's slow progress below.

Keane kept low to the ground, crawling on his belly like a snake beneath the scant cover a ridge of stone gave him. He was suddenly remembering the other times, when the enemy had been the Apache. Fighting Mexicans wasn't much different, and fighting Ortegas was becoming something of a habit—one he'd just as soon break.

He made it to a rocky outcropping and stopped, listening

to Louvel's little rifle sounding more like a firecracker than a real gun. A .22 would kill a man just as dead as a .44 . . . it just took longer. He eased around the back side of the rock and scrambled up the slope, falling behind a clump of sage. Louvel's rifle kept popping across the way, while Santiago and his men replied with real rifles.

Keane hunched and sprinted up the slope, crushing himself into a rocky crevice in full sunlight. His breathing came in hard, short gasps and sweat stung his eyes and salted the corners of his mouth. He'd been away from the army almost four years now and wasn't used to the exertion.

They were still above him, but not so far anymore. He spied a flicker of red and blue among the rocks up there. They were moving to outflank Louvel while trying to locate him. Then a pistol barked and hot stone erupted, stinging his cheek. Keane dropped and swung to his right, firing at a man who had stepped out into the open. His bullet punched the Mexican in the left shoulder and wrenched him around, and his revolver clattered down the rocky slope a few feet.

Louvel's rifle cracked, and somewhere among the rocks a man howled and cussed. The Mexicans were on the move, but hunkered down where he was, Keane could not tell in what direction they were going.

He sucked in a breath and strode up the slope toward the man on the ground clutching a shoulder and groaning. A rifle appeared above and Keane snapped off two quick shots at it. It disappeared, but then a shot came from another direction, burning his thigh. Keane hit the sharp stones and covered his head with his arms as two more shots rang out. He rolled behind a rock, out of range, and examined his leg, finding a shallow gash that ran from just below his hip to a few inches above his knee. It burned like sin and was bleeding heavily, but it wasn't serious.

Then a small slide of stones began cascading down around the rock where he had found cover. They were coming for him. He fired and ducked back. Louvel had squeezed off another shot from a different direction this time. Then a revolver began chattering from across the way. The Mexicans halted their descent and dove for cover.

Keane rolled out. A bullet smashed the rocks just in front of him and he froze as an older man stepped around the shoulder of sandstone with a rifle in his hands. Keane set the revolver down and raised his hands.

"Surrendering will not save you, señor. Nothing will now," the Mexican said with cool certainty. He shouted up the hill. "Santiago! I have the man."

After a moment a face appeared from behind another rock up the slope. "Shoot the bastard," the man ordered. "Shoot him now; then we will finish off the other one, like we should have last night!"

Suddenly a rock whizzed through the air and smacked solidly into the Mexican's jaw. It knocked his head sideways and his finger involuntarily squeezed the trigger. The bullet flew wide. Keane grabbed his revolver and fired.

Santiago and his boys were coming for him when he snatched the Mexican's rifle from where it had fallen and began ratcheting the lever and pulling the trigger. They lit out of there like cats with their tails on fire and disappeared over the ridge. Keane heard the sound of their horses pounding the trail, fading swiftly in the distance.

Weakly, Keane stood, pain scorching his leg. From across the way, Royden Louvel stalked toward him, revolver in hand, his pint-size rifle tucked under his stump. Four bodies lay across the hillside, and three of them were still breathing.

"Ah think the rascals have run off," Louvel called as he descended the slope, rocks clattering ahead of him in small slides with each step he took.

"It appears so," Keane said, scanning the ridge where the Mexicans had vanished.

Louvel stopped to examine one of the Mexicans. "Appears we have us some prisoners."

"I'm sure the sheriff at Tombstone will be delighted. I understand most of the Ortegas have prices on their heads."

"Ah can use a little spending money."

"The cards aren't paying off?"

Louvel continued across the gravelly ground. "Ah'm always short of cash these days, suh. Seems to be my plight since you dammed Yankees stole my inheritance and my livelihood." Suddenly the Southerner went stiff, and the revolver snapped up. "Apache!"

Keane turned as the Indian stepped into view, leading a footsore pony. "Hold up there, Louvel," Keane ordered, his voice ringing with authority of a man used to issuing commands.

Fortunately Louvel had reverted back to long-unused training, too. He held his fire.

Keane looked again, then said, "Nantaje? Is that you?"

"John Russell. It has been many years since we have ridden together."

"Over four." Keane limped the few paces that separated them and the two men shook hands. "You can put that gun down, Louvel. Nantaje and me, we're old friends." He looked at the Indian. "I should have guessed it was you when that rock knocked this one for a loop. You must still be pitching a baseball for the troops."

Nantaje did not smile. "If I had had a gun I would have killed him for you, John Russell."

Louvel came over and Keane introduced them. "Well, what are you doing here, Nantaje? Troops just over the hill? Is that what scared Santiago and his men off?"

The Apache shook his head. "No. No troops. Crook is no longer white chief."

"What happened?" Concern edged Keane's voice. Although he and General Crook had their disagreements, they had enjoyed a friendship common among fighting men.

"Sheridan sent him away."

"Who is in command of the department of Arizona?"

"Miles."

"Miles! Might have known. Miles and Sheridan think alike."

"Gave me my walking papers."

"Not surprised. Miles and Sheridan never did see eye-to-eye with Crook, with him using Apache scouts. Sorry to hear it, Nantaje. You're one crackerjack tracker . . . but what are you doing here?"

"I was on my way to find you when I heard the shots." He paused, glanced at the Southerner, then back at Keane. "I need your help, John Russell. I need it badly."

Chapter Eight

"You know who this is?" Deputy Hank Rader asked, staring into the lifeless eyes of the man tied across the back of the horse.

"Louvel here tells me his name is Armando Ortega."

"Armando Ortega, all right. One of the four Ortega brothers. Geez, Keane. What are you on, a one-man mission to clean up this land of Ortegas?"

He grinned. "I don't go looking for them, Hank, if that's what you mean. There's probably paper on all four of them. I've changed my mind about the rewards. I can use some money to stake me and my friends here. See what you can get for them." He put the dead man and the three who weren't into Rader's care. "You know where to find me."

Rader glanced from Keane to Louvel, and finally at Nantaje, his view lingering suspiciously upon the Apache. "The three of you?"

"When you get the money bring it by. I'll sign whatever papers are necessary."

"John?"

Keane turned back.

"You're limping again."

He touched his thigh where the bullet had burned it and grinned. "Reckon I'm either getting too soft for this land, Hank, or it's getting too hard for me."

Nantaje turned few heads when they stepped into the café. With Fort Huachuca so close by, most folks had become accustomed to the occasional Apache scout in town. Laura Caesar took their orders and when she left, Keane said, "Let me get this straight. Renegade soldiers attacked your village and took your people into Mexico, where they sold them to a man named Gaspar Ortega. And this Ortega, he is somehow related to those four we just brought in. Right?"

"Yes, John Russell. My people are to be put on a train and taken to the Gulf of California. Then a boat will carry them south."

"To Guadalajara," Keane added.

"I came to you, John Russell, because you are a just man. I know what you did for the Apache at the Salt River."

Keane frowned. "That day was a turning point in a lot of people's lives."

Louvel looked curious, but neither Keane nor Nantaje said any more about it. When Laura came by with their meal, Keane borrowed a pencil and a scrap of paper. "Draw it out for me the way you remember it."

Nantaje laid out the town and the land features. "The railroad tracks cross a deep gulch here, just before entering a canyon. It is how they brought us in. I don't know if there is another way in, John Russell.

"The canyon opens up after a mile or two and the town lies beyond." He sketched the primary streets and blocks of buildings approximately where they stood. "These are the cattle pens where they keep the people. Guard towers here, here, and along here. Beacon fires burn all night, but by the early morning hours they burn low and are not tended regularly."

"What about the Gatling guns?" Louvel asked.

"Here and here."

"Watching both ends of town," Keane noted.

"And here they have a cannon and a caisson."

Louvel pondered the layout a moment. "One thing is certain: this man, Gaspar Ortega, has never engaged in any serious fighting. His defenses are all wrong. He would have to move the Gatlings to cover an attack from his flanks, and what does he expect to do with that cannon? Blow holes in his own buildings? It belongs here, on this bit of high ground."

"I agree. I could take the place with a dozen trained soldiers." Keane glanced at the Southerner. "You've taken a particular interest in this. Does that mean you're thinking of coming along?"

"Along? Suh, with only the two of you, what your Apache friend here is proposing to accomplish is sheer suicide. No, indeed. My interests are merely professional. This is the sort of game we played at West Point to sharpen our skills. Ah recall one brash underclassman who was particularly brilliant, if not completely unorthodox. A tactician of the first order. His name was George Armstrong Custer. You may have heard of him."

Keane gave a short laugh and nodded. "Since Little Bighorn, the whole world has heard of Lieutenant Colonel Custer. He was a fine man, a good friend."

"You are right. The whole world has heard of him. My point exactly. Unorthodox. And that is what you must become, Major Keane, if you expect to pull off this little escapade with just the two of you. What about these railroad tracks? Are they still operational?"

"Yes. There is a locomotive with six cars behind it, the kind that carry cattle. Butler says that is how my people will be taken out of the canyon, to the gulf." The Apache's dark eyes shifted to Keane, concern showing in them. "If they get that locomotive moving, John Russell, there is no way we could stop it."

"Probably not. But we could stop it from going any-where."

"How do you propose to do that?" Louvel asked.

Keane put a finger to the map. "Trestle here. What if we blow it before we move into the canyon? Even if they should get the train moving, it won't go any farther than the mouth of the canyon." Keane grinned. "For a West Point-trained tactician, I'm surprised you didn't think of that."

"I did," Louvel said smoothly, his Louisiana feathers unruffled. "But I wonder how much you or our Apache friend know about explosives, and setting charges that would take down a structure engineered to support the weight of a locomotive and ore cars? I learned during the war that the task was more difficult than it appeared. Sometimes all that resulted was a vast plume of smoke and dirt, and when it cleared, the trestle was still standing."

Keane frowned. "What you say is true, Captain. But I know someone who just might be able to help."

Dougal O'Brian clawed at the wrinkled skin beneath his wild white beard, scowling over the bat-wing door. The ancient brand that marked his cheek was itching again, and that always made him surly. O'Brian was a thickset man with ruddy, sunburned skin and tangled eyebrows nearly as untamed as the beard. His face, what could be seen of it, was a collection of scars and old pockmarks. He wore a dingy tan canvas vest, made bulky by everything he carried inside it.

It wasn't only the bothersome scar, put there nearly four decades earlier, that had O'Brian in a foul mood now. Being cantankerous just came naturally to him these days. He usually put it off to growing old, or to his arthritis, or to fool people with no more sense than a rangy three-day-old colt. The West was growing fat with such people. The real reason he was feeling particularly peevish now was because he'd been all night and most of the day without a drink.

O'Brian pushed through the doors and went inside the cantina. A man in a serape, with a black cur of a dog at his feet on the cool adobe floor, sat at one of the tables watching him from under a wide sombrero as he made his way to the bar. Another was sprawled across a table, still clutching an empty bottle of tequila. Whether he was asleep or dead, O'Brian couldn't be sure; in this wild Mexican settlement of Fronteras nothing surprised or shocked him anymore.

A fly buzzed annoyingly at his ear; then something touched his sweaty neck. His hand lashed out with a sharp crack and he grinned at the bloody smear upon his palm.

"Ah, Señor San Patricio! It is good to see you again," the cantina's *patrón* said, coming through a blanket that served as a door to the back room, where the girls were. He was a slender, black-haired fellow with a thin mustache, somewhere between thirty and forty, with an easy smile and wary eyes.

"Tequila, Hernandez, and leave the bottle." Even now, after all these years, he still spoke with a faint Irish accent. It was hardly noticeable in English, but for some reason it made folks look twice when he spoke Spanish. O'Brian reserved his Spanish for those times when it was absolutely necessary.

Hernandez clucked disapprovingly. "You are in a very bad mood today. What has happened?"

O'Brian scowled, scratching at the scar again. "Ignacia kicked me out last night."

"She did? Now I see why you are unhappy. Ignacia, the very flower of womanhood! So sweet and gentle," Hernandez lamented.

"Sweet and gentle? Horse crap. She's a fat old whore years past her prime. Everyone knows that. I turn sixty-five and Ignacia up and leaves me for another man. Here, gimme that bottle." O'Brian spilled it into a glass and tossed it back, smacking his lips. "I needed that."

"You loved her? Yes?"

"Oh, yes, I loved her. Loved her hard and often, and about every way a man can imagine."

Hernandez chuckled. "And that is why you miss her?"

"Willing women are as common as fleas on a dog in this country. Hell, you got a roomful of them yourself back there."

"Then why is it you are sad, señor?"

"I'll tell you why." O'Brian took another long pull at the glass and filled it to the rim a second time. "It's because Ignacia has the damnedest cache of tequila and whiskey any man has ever laid eyes upon." He shook his head. "Sure gonna miss that woman."

Hernandez chuckled softly.

O'Brian reached inside his vest for a cigar.

"Señor! What is all that?"

"What, this?" O'Brian pulled a stick of dynamite from an inside pocket. "You don't have to worry about this, Hernandez. It's safe enough. See?" He whacked it a couple of times on the bar and grinned. "Harmless."

Hernandez sucked in a breath. O'Brian laughed, struck a match, and lit his cigar. "See, you can even burn the stuff and it won't go off." He fanned the flame under the dynamite until Hernandez looked as though he were about to pop.

"Señor! No, no! Do not do that!"

Dougal O'Brian laughed. A shadow darkened the doorway. He glanced over and his smile turned to a frown. "Here comes trouble," he said quietly.

"Perhaps not. Maybe they just want to drink."

Francisco and Ruben Ortega drew up in the dim cantina

and looked around. Wordlessly, the older man pointed at a table with his quirt. His son, Ruben, came to the bar and asked for tequila. Hernandez gave him a bottle, two glasses, and pocketed his money.

They settled down at the table, talking low and glancing at the door from time to time.

"Trouble on two legs, that boy is," O'Brian observed softly, taking another drink.

"You don't cause trouble, they don't cause trouble. Everybody is happy, and that is the way I like it," Hernandez replied, equally subdued.

"Me? Cause trouble?" O'Brian pretended he was hurt.

Hernandez laughed quietly. "You particularly, Señor San Patricio."

"Don't call me that."

"Whatever you say, Señor O'Brian."

"That's better." He looked over his shoulder, then back at Hernandez. "They seem to be waiting for someone. Wonder who?"

"It is not your business, señor. I'd advise you not to make it so."

"Wouldn't think of it." Just the same, O'Brian glanced at the old caplock revolver shoved under his belt, checking that each nipple was still covered with a cap.

"They say Casa Rita is beautiful this year. They have had rain and everything is green and the flowers, they grow everywhere," Hernandez offered.

"Don't know. Ain't been to Casa Rita since old Pedro Marcos sold me that blind mule. Fact is, after I finished with Marcos, the town's people run me out. Promised me a necktie party if I ever show my face there again," O'Brian replied.

"How many towns have you been run out of, señor?"

"I don't know. Stopped counting years ago. But I've about used 'em all up here in this part of Mexico."

"There is always the *Estados Unidos*."

98

O'Brian spat on Hernandez's red mud floor and said, "I'd sooner sleep with a skunk than go back to the States." He touched the old brand upon his cheek and his eyes went smoky.

"That was a long time ago, señor," Hernandez said as if he understood what O'Brian was thinking.

"Not long enough for my liking."

The old Irishman took another long swallow and the two men fell silent, O'Brian brooding in his glass, rolling it thoughtfully between the palms of his hands. "I did go back a couple times," he said finally.

"And?" Hernandez prompted, reaching for the bottle and pouring himself a drink. "What happened?"

"Yankees came down and took over the country. So I left again. Came back to Mexico."

"You speak of your Civil War? You fought in it?"

O'Brian studied the glass a moment. "I fought for what I believed in. The hope of the people for an independent country. But that scoundrel Lincoln dashed that dream, too." O'Brian gave a short laugh. "Well, Lincoln got what was coming to him."

There was a commotion out in the street. Hernandez and O'Brian moved to the dingy window. A young man in a blue uniform was being hauled across the street by a gang of Mexicans. His clothing was torn and his face was purple and swollen about the eyes and nose. His lip was about twice normal size, and as they got closer, O'Brian could see the dried blood down the front of his military blouse. Then he saw the girl. She ran out from an alleyway and began pummeling one of the Mexicans. A third man suddenly appeared, snagged her by the wrist, and pulled her away, grabbing her arms.

"Francisco!" one of them called.

The older man and his son rose from the table and stepped outside into the harsh sunlight. The men released the soldier but kept him covered.

"Is this the North American?" Francisco demanded.

"Yes. He is the one."

Francisco strode out and stalked around the young man, his dark eyes glaring out from beneath the wide hat. "So, it is you!" The quirt shot out and cracked across the man's face.

"Father! No, don't!"

Francisco grabbed the girl and held her before the man. "You are the one who did this to my daughter? Defiled her so that now she carries your bastard child?"

The soldier shook the wool from his head and cradled his jaw, fresh blood trickling through his fingers. "I love Delicia, Señor Ortega."

"It is true, Father. And I love Harrison."

"Shut up! You are no more than a child. What do you know of love? Only enough to copulate with this North American dog. Even the cats in our barns know that much! You bring disgrace upon our family!"

O'Brian glanced at Hernandez, grinning. "I've been in a fix like that a time or two. Never got caught. That boy's in for a hard time."

"*Sí.* I fear his voice is destined to climb an octave or two," Hernandez remarked, shaking his head.

"If he's lucky enough to live through it. Come to think of it, maybe living would be unlucky." O'Brian laughed, feeling little remorse for the young man. Had he not been a soldier in the service of a country O'Brian hated, he might have conjured up a bit more sympathy. Absently, he began stroking the scar buried beneath the wild beard.

"Your name, it is what?" the Mexican demanded.

"Ridere. Harrison Ridere."

"Ridere? So you make out like a bull with my daughter. You know what we do to bulls to cool their blood?" Francisco Ortega laughed. "I see you do." He pulled out his bowie knife from a belt sheath. "We make them steers."

Hernandez's face grew pale. "Sweet Mother Mary. I do not want to watch this." He looked away, but either a natural curiosity or a fascination with the macabre brought his eyes back to the window and the scene out on the street.

Francisco's men had closed in, surrounding him as the soldier cast about for an avenue of escape. Suddenly they lunged and took him by the arms.

"No! Don't do this!" the soldier cried, struggling in their grasp. They had him, and at Francisco's command wrestled him to the street and started unbuckling his belt and tugging at his trousers.

"Father, don't. Please don't do this to him!"

Francisco tossed his daughter aside, then turned the knife toward Ridere, sunlight sliding along the long, polished blade, glinting off its honed edge. "Now you will pay for what you have done."

Ridere kicked out. Two more of Francisco's men grabbed his legs, spreading them.

"This is going to be bloody," O'Brian said, his spirit suddenly heavy, torn between an unforgiving heart and a streak of sympathy that went out to the desperate soldier.

"Too bad there is no one here to help the young man," Hernandez replied, his eyes glued now.

O'Brian shook his head and looked away. "It's not my problem." His gut wrenched into knots as he listened to the soldier plead for mercy.

"You have to believe me. I love her! I have risked everything for your daughter, Francisco," Ridere implored, terror ringing in his shrill voice.

If he had only been someone else, O'Brian told himself, trying to ease his own conscience at not stepping in and helping. Almost anyone else. But a soldier of the United States . . .

"I have even deserted my post to be with her, Francisco! What more can I do to prove my love?" he tried one final time.

O'Brian's head snapped up, eyes narrowing.

"He is a deserter," Hernandez noted, glancing at his friend. "Just like you, Señor San Patricio."

"Told you not to call me that anymore." Dougal O'Brian scowled and thought it over a second. He took a stick of dynamite from his vest pocket, turned a twist of fuse around his forefinger, held it with his thumb, and lit it. Holding it behind his back, he stepped out into the street.

"Francisco!"

The Mexican glanced up, his knife poised and about to slash down.

"You've had your fun. Now I'll be asking you to step away from the lad and let him up."

Francisco narrowed an eye at him. "O'Brian, isn't it?"

"That be the name." The four on the ground trying to contain the struggling man had their hands full. The son, Ruben, was armed, but his hand was not near the revolver. There was one with a rifle, levered easily over his shoulder and held by the barrel. Another wore a revolver, but presently he was clutching the lapels of his vest and grinning. O'Brian wasn't put off guard by their casualness. These were murderers, every one of them wanted in Mexico and the United States.

"You don't want to get involved here," Francisco said, sounding willing to overlook his indiscretion.

"You're right about that. But somehow I figured it was time to step in, so I guess I'm already involved. I heard what the fellow done to your daughter. I reckon his only real crime was getting caught. He only done what comes natural to a man. You and me, we both got little bastards running all over this country. Let him up and I'll buy you and your boys a drink. Who knows, this soldier boy might turn out to be a half-decent son-in-law, given a chance. One thing for sure, you go through with this, Delicia's gonna hate you the rest of your life for it."

Francisco considered and stood, knife still in his gun hand. "Chico, Moises, what think you of his words?"

The one with the rifle shifted his weight and said, "I think after we finish with the North American, we teach the old man the same lesson."

O'Brian felt the heat of the fuse close to his fingers.

Francisco grinned and nodded his head. "And you, Moises?"

Moises's thumbs stroked his leather lapels as his sweaty grin widened and the drooping mustache hiked up at the ends. "I will hold the old man down as you do the cutting, Francisco."

The Mexican leader laughed. "My friends do not seem to want to drink with you, Señor O'Brian."

"That's a real shame, Francisco." The fire was nearly to his fingers. O'Brian saw the rifle slide slowly off of Chico's shoulder. Ridere had stopped his struggling, and like the men holding him, seemed to be waiting to see what would happen next.

Fire kissed his fingers and seared his skin. O'Brian released the fuse and started counting to himself.

Francisco's easy tone turned flinty. "I think maybe you have fought your last war this time, Señor O'Brian."

O'Brian frowned. "Sorta looks that way, *amigo.*" He twisted toward Ruben. "Here, sonny boy, catch!"

Instinctively, Ruben stuck out a hand and snatched the stick of dynamite from the air. Its sputtering fuse was nearly to the cap. His eyes bulged and he gave a startled cry and flung it in the air.

The Mexicans jumped and threw their arms up at the explosion and the concussion. That was all the edge O'Brian needed. He stabbed for his revolver, swung to his left, and fired. Chico was already swinging the rifle when O'Brian's bullet parted his eyes and blew his skull out the back of his head. Moises grabbed for his revolver. He buckled at the waist as the Irishman's second shot landed a punch to his stomach.

Then everyone was moving, grabbing for guns, scrambling for cover. O'Brian dove to the street, rolled, and snapped a shot at one of the men on the ground. Francisco's revolver cleared leather. O'Brian fired, missed, and felt the tug of the Ortega's bullet at his left arm. There was no pain, only a dull thump, as if he'd been kicked by a mule. O'Brian fired again. Francisco leaped over a watering trough, slipped, and half fell into it, then scrambled out and fell behind it. Ruben was sprinting across the street. One of the men on the ground finally had a gun out. O'Brian shot him through the throat.

Ridere snatched the gun from the dead Mexican's fingers and killed one of the men who had held his legs. O'Brian finished off the other, and then his revolver was empty. Ridere tried to stand, tripped on the trousers still down around his ankles, grabbed them up by the belt, and fired three quick shots into the trough to keep Francisco's head down.

"Let's get the hell out of here!" O'Brian shouted, rolling to his knees.

Ridere flung himself bare-assed down the street, all the while trying to yank his pants up as he hobbled like a drunken sailor for one of the horses. O'Brian made a dash for his own horse. Somehow Ridere got his trousers up high enough to straddle the animal, and the two men lit out for the edge of town with Francisco and Ruben sending lead and curses after them.

Chapter Nine

O'Brian winced and ground his teeth.

"Hurt bad?" Ridere paused in cleaning the crusted blood from around the wound, then gently pressed the damp cloth to the clot, trying to soften it. They'd ridden hard for most of an hour. Dougal O'Brian had cut across country and finally turned onto a hidden trail he knew of. The tortuous way wound far back into the hills and then dipped into a little boxed canyon that Ridere figured would be impossible to find. It was rough country, the kind of hard, rocky land where only an Apache scout could trail them. But O'Brian seemed to know exactly where he was going and finally reined to a stop next to a clear stream that flowed from the barren mountain peaks to the west.

"Damn right it hurts, but you finish up. I've lived through worse."

Ridere wiped away the blood, then examined the wound. It was a big enough hole. A .45 never made a minor wound, but it was clean. The bullet had passed completely through the thick muscle just below the elbow, not hitting bone nor cutting an artery. O'Brian was going to live, but he'd be sore and hampered for a couple of weeks.

"Haven't had a chance to thank you yet for stepping in."

"A man my age ought to have learned not to stick his nose where it don't belong," O'Brian said with a snarl.

Ridere grimaced. "Why did you do it?"

"Not sure yet. But it will come to me directly." He stared at Ridere, studying him a moment. "Did you tell Francisco the straight of it back there? You run off from the army for that girl?"

"Delicia?" He made a small smirk. "She was part of it."

"And the other part?"

Ridere shrugged. "You might say I got tired of sleeping in the guardhouse, and sleeping with Delicia looked a whole lot better."

O'Brian laughed. "A man after my own heart."

"Maybe, but not very smart. Now I've got the army looking for me up north, and Francisco hunting my hide here. Seems I got myself backed into a tight corner with no where to go."

"There is always a way to go," O'Brian said. "Sometimes it just takes some searching to find it."

Ridere glanced at the Mexican's horse he had stolen. "Maybe there's something in those saddlebags we can use for a bandage?"

Harrison Ridere was a handsome man: tall, youthfully thin, with sandy hair, wide shoulders, and a narrow waist to be envied by anyone much over forty. O'Brian frowned down at his own thick middle, remembering his youth. He had left County Cork, Ireland for Canada almost half a century ago, a strapping young man bound for adventure and a career in the British Army. It felt a lifetime to him. No, two lifetimes! To get from the cool, lush forests of Canada to the burning wastelands of northern Mexico was more of an adventure than most men would care to experience.

"Nothing for a bandage," Ridere said coming back, carrying a bottle. "But I found this."

"Tequila?"

"Nearly full." Ridere twisted out the cork and took a whiff. His face wrinkled. "Strong stuff. It will help disinfect that bullet wound."

"Aye, but only a wee bit. I'll not have you wasting that on my outside when my insides need it worse . . . to kill the pain, you understand."

Ridere laughed and poured the tequila into the wound. O'Brian howled. "That will be enough of that," he said, snatching the bottle away and tipping it up. Ridere washed O'Brian's bandanna in the stream, wrung it out, and wrapped the Irishman's arm.

"You ought to have a doctor look at that."

"More likely to find a virgin in a whorehouse than a doctor in these parts." He passed the bottle.

Ridere took a small drink that puckered his lips and drew moisture to his eyes. "This stuff has the sting of a scorpion." He passed it back. "There is a doctor at Fort Huachuca."

O'Brian scowled past the upturned bottle. "I'll not be crawling off to no army post for help, not even if old Francisco had put a bullet through both my arms." He shoved the bottle into Ridere's fist. "Damn that *hombre!* I'll pay him back for this!"

"Francisco Ortega is not a man to trifle with," Ridere warned. "He's meaner than a riled badger, and he's got three brothers and who knows how many nephews. All good with a gun, most wanted by the law in both countries."

"Tell me something I don't know," O'Brian said gruffly.

"Even the army is on the lookout for them. They attacked a small detachment last spring and took a twelve-pounder fieldpiece and two Gatling guns. There were five thousand rounds of ammunition for the Gatlings. We trailed them down into Mexico, but lost them in the

Patagonias. Crook ordered us back. Said he had enough trouble running down Apache without sending men off after Mexican bandits, too. But I think he just didn't want to involve the United States in a border dispute with the Mexican government."

"Gatling guns?" O'Brian's brow furrowed. "Wonder what the Ortegas wanted Gatling guns for?" He snorted and took the bottle from Ridere's hand. "Probably has them stashed at their stronghold, an old ghost town called Montaña la Plata."

"The Ortegas have a stronghold?"

"It's an abandoned mining camp. A couple unlucky North Americans took some silver out of there a while back, but the big mines down around Guadalajara caught wind of it and ran them out. They put a lot of money into developing it, even built themselves a railroad to the Gulf of California so they could haul in supplies from the steamboats that ran back and forth from their main operation. But the silver played out after a year or two and the Guadalajara companies abandoned the place. That's when Gaspar Ortega and his brothers moved in and took over. There's only one way in or out, and that's through the canyon where they put down the rails. I don't think the old road is in use anymore, but I can't say for sure. It's been a while since I've been there."

"You've been there?"

"Worked for the mines a long time ago, before the Ortegas moved in."

"What did the mine owners say about the Ortegas taking over Montaña la Plata?"

O'Brian frowned. "They're all crooks, but I reckon there is some honor among thieves after all. They got themselves some kind of agreement, the Ortegas and the mine owners. I'm not sure what it is, but rumor has it there's good money to be made in slaving."

"Slaving?"

O'Brian shrugged and winced from the fire the motion brought to his arm. He scowled at the makeshift bandage, dousing the frown with another generous dose of tequila. "Those silver mines, they need people to work them—lots of people. And no sane man will work in the conditions some of them mines are in. People don't live long digging Guadalajara silver. But slaves, well, I reckon they have no say-so in the matter."

Ridere accepted the bottle. He tried it again, cautiously this time, then a bit more enthusiastically. "It sort of loses its bite after a couple swallows."

"Mellows right out," O'Brian agreed, taking it and slugging back another round.

"What about the Mexican authorities? What are they doing to stop them?"

O'Brian dragged a sleeve across his mouth and chin. "They don't seem to much care what the Ortegas are up to. Leastwise, not enough to try to ferret them out of their mountain fort. Besides, you got to understand the nature of politics down here. A couple hundred pesos in the right palms grease the skids real good."

Ridere took another drink.

"Sorta grows on you, don't it?" O'Brian said, slurring the words slightly. "I can hardly feel the arm anymore." That was a lie, but he wasn't going to let on to this young runaway soldier how badly it really did hurt.

They talked on into the afternoon, waiting out the heat in the shade of the canyon. They finished off the bottle of tequila, and when Ridere stood he stabbed out a foot to brace himself. "Whoa, what was that?"

"Probably just one of them baby earthy-quakes." O'Brian giggled.

"Good thing. For a second there I thought it was me."

O'Brian staggered to his horse.

"Where we headed now?"

"I got a place up in the hills. We'll be safe there until my arm mends."

"Live by yourself?"

O'Brian cast him a narrow look. "Course I do . . . now." He thought of Ignacia and regretted losing her, but he regretted losing access day or night to her pantry of tequila and whiskey even more. "I'm the only one who can put up with me for very long."

Ridere took up the reins of the Mexican horse, hauling himself clumsily into the saddle. "After you mend, then what?"

"Then I'm gonna go pay Francisco a visit."

"Alone?"

"You can ride along if you want."

Ridere shook his head. "No, thank you, Mr. O'Brian. If I'm gonna pay any Ortega a visit, it will be Delicia."

"Then I reckon I'll be going alone. Faced bigger odds in my life, I have." His finger moved instinctively to the branded scar upon his cheek.

"What's that?"

"What?"

"You keep fingering it as if maybe it bothers you. Looks like a nasty scar there."

"It's nothing," O'Brian said, quickly combing the shaggy hair down over the mark. He turned away and clucked his horse ahead.

Chapter Ten

"We could use your help."

Louvel laughed and shook his head. "No, suh, not Ah. Ah've fought for my cause."

"Is ours so much different than yours was?" Nantaje asked.

Louvel thought. "No, Ah suppose not. Just the same, Ah've done my fighting and made my sacrifice." He lifted the stump slightly. "Ah am sorry, but these days there has got to be something more in it for me to make it worth putting my neck on the line again."

"Like honor?"

"Yes, Major Keane. Honor, for one."

"And how about silver for two?"

Keane and Louvel looked at the Apache. "What about silver, suh?"

"More than can fill a wagon. That's what one of the men told me."

No one spoke for a moment.

Keane said, "That would explain Gaspar Ortega wanting all that artillery."

"And the men, John Russell."

"Exactly how many men are we talking about here?" Louvel inquired.

"I saw maybe twenty. But there were some more. I don't know exactly."

"Twenty plus, and we'd be only three." Louvel shook his head. "It still sounds like suicide to me."

Nantaje looked out the window and pointed at a freight wagon rolling up the street. "How much silver could a wagon that size haul, John Russell?"

"My guess would be maybe a quarter of a million dollars' worth." He glanced at the reluctant Southerner. "More than enough to rebuild a shattered past. Maybe buy a nice plantation house and, oh, four or five thousand acres to go along with it?"

Louvel's dark eyes narrowed. "Sheer suicide."

"Maybe."

Deputy Hank Rader stepped through the doorway and came to their table. "I did some checking for you, John. Those four you brought in today, and the three you hauled in over their saddles last week, the rewards amount to a little over seven hundred and fifty dollars."

Keane gave a low whistle. "Here I've been trying to claw silver up out of the ground when all the while the real money to be made lay in rounding up members of the Ortega family."

"Looks like it. Only trouble is, the rewards have all been issued by six different municipalities, including the U.S. Army and Mexico."

"What you're saying is, there is no reward money."

"No. What I'm saying, John, is that it's going to take the city of Tombstone a while to collect it all. Then there will be some clerical costs involved, which will have to come out of whatever monies are paid out."

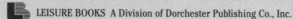

GET YOUR 4
FREE* BOOKS NOW—
A VALUE BETWEEN
$16 AND $20

Mail the Free* Book Certificate Today!

FREE* BOOKS
CERTIFICATE!

YES! I want to subscribe to the Leisure Western Book Club. Please send me my 4 FREE* BOOKS. Then, each month, I'll receive the four newest Leisure Western Selections to preview FREE* for 10 days. If I decide to keep them, I will pay the Special Member's Only discounted price of just $3.36 each, a total of $13.44 ($14.50 US in Canada). This saves me between $3 and $6 off the bookstore price. There are no shipping, handling or other charges.* There is no minimum number of books I must buy and I may cancel the program at any time. In any case, the 4 FREE* BOOKS are mine to keep—at a value of between $17 and $20!

*In Canada, add $5.00 Canadian shipping and handling per order for first shipment. For all subsequent shipments to Canada the cost of membership in the Book Club is $14.50 US, which includes $7.50 shipping and handling per month. All payments must be made in US currency.

Name _____

Address _____

City_____ State_____ Country_____

Zip_____ Telephone_____

Tear here and mail your FREE* book card today!

If under 18, parent or guardian must sign. Terms, prices and conditions subject to change. Subscription subject to acceptance. Leisure Books reserves the right to reject any order or cancel any subscription.

Get Four Books Totally FREE* — A Value between $16 and $20

Tear here and mail your FREE* book card today!

PLEASE RUSH MY FOUR FREE* BOOKS TO ME RIGHT AWAY!

LeisureWestern Book Club
P.O. Box 6613
Edison, NJ 08818-6613

AFFIX STAMP HERE

Keane frowned. "How long?"

Rader shrugged. "Two, maybe three months."

Rader left after the men finished their meal. Outside, the sun had lost some of its heat and scattered clouds had begun to gather. Keane hoped for rain, but wasn't going to hold his breath for it. It had been weeks since any moisture had fallen to settle the dust.

"Reckon this is where we part company, Louvel."

"Ah still say it's a fool's errand, Major Keane."

"Maybe. I have been known to play the fool from time to time. Thanks again for your help." Keane offered his hand.

Louvel took it. "Never thought I'd be shaking the hand of a damned Yankee. Good luck."

They dropped by the livery stable. Nantaje used his army pay to buy a hackamore bit and a blanket for his pony, and afterward at the general store a well-used 1860 Army Colt for three dollars. Keane convinced the merchant to throw in powder, balls, and enough caps for fifty shots for the old revolver, and bought two boxes of .44s for his own revolver and rifle. He rounded it out with some canned beans, coffee, and a new pair of britches.

It was nearly dark when Nantaje and Keane saddled up and rode out of Tombstone. Royden Louvel was astride his horse, waiting for them at the edge of town.

"You two are still going through with this scheme?" the Southerner asked.

"Reckon I've always been a sucker for a good cause. Nantaje's people need help, and there doesn't seem to be anyone else around interested in giving it."

He considered the two of them, then shook his head. "Don Quixote de la Mancha, and his faithful sidekick, Sancho Panza."

"Maybe."

"Suicide."

"So you have pointed out."

"Sheer suicide."

"If that is what you really believe, what made you change your mind, Captain Louvel?"

"What makes you think Ah have?"

Keane pointed at the Southerner's horse. "You're all packed up and ready to go. And you haven't been waiting here just to remind us of the hopelessness of our job."

Louvel frowned. "You are quite perceptive, for a damned Yankee."

"And you care more than you want to let on, for a bitter Graycoat."

"It's the silver."

"Is that all?"

"That is correct, suh."

"Uh-huh."

"We are losing the daylight, John Russell."

Keane looked back at the Southerner. "Well, Captain Louvel, if it is the silver you want, come join us in our quest for silver windmills."

"If Ah have ciphered it out correctly, and taking their numbers to be about twenty-five, Ah reckon the odds are eight to one . . . against us."

Keane stirred their campfire with a stick. "Are those staying odds for a gambling man like yourself, Captain Louvel?"

"Not hardly, suh."

"Except when a wagonload of silver is the prize?"

"That does figure into the calculations."

They heard Nantaje coming into their camp. The Apache emerged from the darkness and dropped an armful of firewood. "Perimeter is secure, John Russell. If Santiago Ortega is following us, he's keeping well back."

"What makes you think he would follow us?" Louvel asked.

"It's what I would do."

"Perhaps he is more concerned with breaking his family out of jail than following us."

"Maybe."

The ex-Confederate filled his coffee cup and leaned back against his saddle. "Ah am curious about this man whom you wish to enlist. This Dougal O'Brian. What makes you think he can help, even if he could be convinced to join a group of men bound to commit suicide?"

"You're going to like O'Brian," Keane said. "You two think alike. He hates the United States just about as much as you do. He was with Zachary Taylor's army to fight the Mexican-American war, but before war was officially declared, O'Brian swam the Rio Grande to help Santa Anna."

"A San Patricio? Ah have heard of them."

"He was branded as a deserter but escaped hanging on a technicality. When the South seceded, O'Brian enlisted to fight the North."

"A Patriot!"

"When I met him he was busy tearing up the track and blowing bridges between Nashville and Louisville. He was right handy with the dynamite—only it wasn't dynamite back then but good old black powder those Johnny Rebs were using. They disrupted our supply lines real good.

"We ambushed a Confederate cavalry setting charges to a bridge near Cheatham. O'Brian was wounded and our company surgeon took care of his wounds while the others were sent off to Libby Prison. In spite of his bluster, Dougal O'Brian was an alright fellow, and a wonderful chess player. We got along pretty well considering I was a Federal officer . . . and O'Brian being much like yourself, Captain." Keane laughed. "He once paid me the biggest compliment a man like O'Brian could give. Said I was the only decent officer in the whole damned Federal army."

Louvel smiled thinly, his black eyes watching Keane.

"Sometime during those weeks of recovery O'Brian told

me he had a place down in Mexico, and he intended to return to it after the war. Well, the war ended and I forgot about O'Brian. Then I was assigned to the department of Arizona under General Crook and I ran across Dougal about five years ago while on patrol in the Sierra Madres along the border. He was blasting for silver or gold with a couple of Mexican miners."

Keane grew silent a moment. When he spoke next his voice held a note of bitterness. "After I left the army, I looked O'Brian up and he showed me how to use dynamite to 'engineer' a hole in the side of a mountain. He's got a cabin south of here. With any luck, tomorrow we'll find him at home."

After almost a week, Harrison Ridere was ready to bid farewell to Dougal O'Brian and his tiny cluttered cabin at the end of a box canyon. The place gave him the shakes, anyway. Looking out the window now, Ridere mused that living a hermit's life all these years must be the reason O'Brian had accumulated enough clutter to properly outfit a junkyard. But he had to wonder about a man who kept crates of explosives around. Explosives by themselves didn't bother Ridere. It was the way O'Brian stored and used them that was strange. The wooden boxes were everywhere. They supported his table and served as chairs. His bed was propped up off the floor on four Nobel Dynamite crates. When he had looked inside one, he was shocked to discover it was still filled with explosives! There were more outside, in a shed, stored with the blasting caps. Ridere mused over what would happen to this box canyon if a bolt of lightning should happen to find that shed.

Surprisingly, Harrison and O'Brian had proved companionable, and O'Brian was going out of his way to be civil. The old Irishman lived a lonely life, and visitors were few and far between. He spoke longingly of Ignacia, his most recent flame extinguished beneath the cold waters of his deep-seated anger. He claimed it was only her well-supplied larder of whiskey and tequila that he really missed, but Ridere figured that was a lie.

Harrison had not yet learned why O'Brian harbored bitter feelings toward the army and the United States, but whatever had happened, it had happened long ago. And it had something to do with the *D* branded into his right cheek. He knew the meaning of that. The army no longer treated deserters so harshly, thank God. But there had been a time not so long ago when a deserter, if not hanged, at the very least went away forever branded for all the world to see. The beard only partly covered it up. Ridere unconsciously touched his cheek, thinking of his own desertion, and knowing that if it had been another time, it could have happened to him. He wondered how he would feel then, if it had.

"I think the time has come for me to pull out of here, Dougal," Ridere said, turning from the window where the canyon opened to catch the rising sun.

O'Brian was frying bacon on the cookstove. "Is that smart? Francisco will be looking for you, and so will the army."

"Figure it's time to be moving on. Maybe California will be far enough away from both of them."

"You'll have to change your name or the army will find you."

"Maybe." Ridere filled his cup with coffee and sat at the battered wooden table. "Wouldn't be the first time a man had to do that."

"I've known a few in my day." O'Brian brought over the frying pan and scraped bacon and scrambled eggs onto their plates. He favored the wounded arm, but a mere bullet hole wasn't enough to stop the Irishman. They ate, and when they finished O'Brian sat there picking his teeth with a splinter.

"Is O'Brian your real name?"

"It is for a fact."

"I take it they caught up with you then, before you had a chance to change it."

He glanced up, then nodded. "They did for a fact." He stroked the beard above the brand.

"When did it happen?" Ridere might have been walking on thin ice, bringing up a past that was plainly painful for the older man, but his curiosity was piqued.

O'Brian thought it over. "Mex-American war."

Ridere figured the years in his head. "That was more than forty years ago."

O'Brian nodded. "Aye, it was, but I remember it just like it was last month."

"How did it happen?"

"Ever hear of the San Patricios?"

Ridere thought, then shook his head.

"Well, not many have these days. 'Specially young people like yourself. The Mexicans called us the *Batallion de San Patricio*. The Saint Patrick Battalion." O'Brian stood and put his plate into a pail on the floor. "We were just some men who got fed up with the way the army was treating us. Mostly Irish, but there were some others. You see, when General Zachary Taylor's Army of Observation arrived at the Mexican border just before the war broke out, Major General Pedro de Ampudia let it be known that there was money, property, and citizenship to be had in Mexico for any soldier who wanted to come over and fight for them. So we went."

"Money and property were what made you do it?"

"Partly. You see, General Santa Anna had himself a real top-notch army. It was well provisioned, with professional officers that didn't take to flogging their soldiers, or staking them spread-eagle and half naked under a burning sun for the smallest offenses. But it was more than that. You got to understand, the Irish were at the bottom of the heap when it came to the U.S. Army. They still are. Most soldiers weren't even American citizens. Some had come down from Canada after walking away from the British Army. It was just a job to them—us—and the working conditions weren't very good."

O'Brian went silent for a moment. "But there was a more important part of it."

"What was that?"

"Most of us were Catholics; Catholics in a Protestant army that didn't care a whit about us. And here we were marching down to fight Santa Anna's army—a Catholic army! Well, we just didn't think it right to be shooting our brothers down here while the army we were fighting for was treating us like dogs. So a bunch of us swam the Rio Grande and took up Ampudia's offer to join with Santa Anna's army."

"Now that you mention it, I think I did hear something about the deserters of the Mexican-American war. Never knew what they were called. Didn't they catch up with you down around Mexico City?"

"Aye, that they did. At a place called Churubusco. Finally overran our position and took us captive, they did. Robert E. Lee and U. S. Grant were there, too. Young officers then, I forget their ranks. Anyway, they tried us for deserters, and hanged most of us. We had to watch, and to dig their graves. Me and eleven others had our sentences reduced to flogging and branding. But all the others . . ." O'Brian's voice cracked and he looked away. "Fine men they were, every one of them. Like brothers to me, they were." His eyes glistened when he looked back.

"Why didn't they hang you?"

O'Brian was staring at nothing in particular and Ridere figured he was seeing the past. "I was just luckier than most," he began slowly. "You see, I swam that Mexican river a few days before war was declared. It was only those men who deserted after the war began who got their necks stretched. For us who left before, deserting wasn't a capital offense. Just a branding, flogging offense. Afterward, I stayed down in Mexico. Only been back over the border a couple times since."

"A lot's changed since then," Ridere said.

"I know."

"Dougal, you don't really want to go after Francisco alone. That would be like sticking your neck in that noose your fellow San Patricios wore all those years ago."

O'Brian did not reply.

"I'm thinking of making for Tombstone, Dougal. Why don't you ride along with me? Nobody here for you right now."

"Tombstone? What in hell is in Tombstone that would make you risk running into the army?"

Ridere grinned. "Her name is Ellie, and she runs the bathhouse. Why, Ellie is the cutest little filly—"

"Ellie?" O'Brian interrupted. "I thought you was in love with Delicia Ortega?"

"I am in love with Delicia . . . when I'm with Delicia. In Tombstone, I love Ellie. Down in Nogales, there is this wild little hellion named Consuela. I'll tell you, Dougal, Consuela has more energy than a wagonload of dynamite." He closed his eyes and shivered slightly, remembering. "Then there is Ramona of Tucson. Ramona has this little thing she does with her tongue that—"

"I don't want to hear no more 'bout it," O'Brian proclaimed, throwing up his hand. "I'll have to go crawling on my hands and knees to Ignacia pleading for her to take me back if you don't stop it." He gave a leering grin. "You're a regular Romeo, ain't you? I should have let Francisco have you."

Ridere laughed. "I'll be forever in your debt for your well-timed arrival, Dougal. So why don't you ride with me to Tombstone? I know lots of girls. We can have us a real good time. That seems to me to be a lot more attractive proposition than getting yourself all shot to pieces going after Francisco."

O'Brian scratched at the chin hidden beneath his beard and closed one eye, as if that helped him to think. "Lots of girls, you say?"

"I know at least three darlings who work at the Bird Cage Theater."

"Ooh. I hear them girls are something else."

"Hotter than firecrackers."

He glanced around the cabin, taking a quick survey of the place. "Ain't got a whole lot here to worry about, except my dynamite."

"Unless it gets struck by lightning, this place will still be standing when you get back."

O'Brian looked at his bandaged arm. "Reckon Francisco will keep. I can always pay him back for this later."

"If that's important to you."

"It is," O'Brian snapped.

Ridere shrugged. "You do what you want, Dougal. As for me, I'm going to Tombstone; then it's off to California." The young soldier looked down at himself and frowned. "'Course, I'll have to find me some different clothes. I wouldn't be exactly inconspicuous in this uniform, not in a town like Tombstone so near to Huachuca."

"Come again with the name of that fort?"

"Huachuca."

"What's it? Wa . . . Wachuka?"

"Huachuca . . . Huachuca, Huachuca, Huachuca!"

"Well, God bless you." O'Brian said and grinned mischievously.

Ridere had been slicked into that one, and he didn't take well to being toyed with. His temper exploded and his fist came up, but O'Brian was quicker, and suddenly Ridere was staring down the barrel of the Irishman's .44.

"Ease back, boy. If we're gonna ride together, you'd best

get used to my way of funning around. If you can't handle it, then it's best you saddle up and leave without me."

Ridere stood there breathing hard, the gun a blur before his eyes. His head cleared and he said, "Sorry, Dougal. Sometimes I fly off the handle. Don't even know when I'm doing it."

"A temper like that will land you in the stockades quicker than eggs through a hen," O'Brian replied evenly, the revolver still ready.

Ridere gave a small grin. "It already has. One reason I skipped out. I only told Francisco I deserted because of Delicia, hoping he'd let me go."

"Not that one. Not Francisco. He's like the Mexican wolf. When he gets you between his jaws, he don't stop shaking until you're dead meat." O'Brian eased down the hammer and shoved the revolver under his belt.

A wave of relief flooded Ridere as the gun disappeared. "My offer still stands, Dougal."

"And I'm gonna take you up on it." O'Brian began gathering his belongings. "I know a little place where you can buy some decent clothes. Like you say, you can't be strutting down the main street of Tombstone wearing them army blues."

Ridere went back to the window. The morning shadows had shrunk back toward the surrounding hills. "When do you want to leave?"

"We can go today if you want."

Ridere was anxious to be away from all this dynamite. "Today will be good." He stared out the window. Riders had appeared in the distance. "You expecting company, Dougal?"

"Company?" O'Brian stepped to the window and squinted. "No." He grabbed a shotgun from the corner, broke open the action, and fetched up a handful of shells from a leather pouch. "You go out the back door and wait behind the cabin. No reason for them to know there are two of us."

Ridere snatched up the revolver he'd taken from the Mexican and slipped outside. O'Brian went out the front door and waited where the sun was hot upon the hard-packed ground and glared off the shimmering heat rising off the land. He shaded his eyes as the riders came closer and reined in.

"John Keane? That you?"

"Good to see you again, Dougal."

"Why, it is you. I never expected a visit from the only decent Federal officer in all of U.S. Grant's army. Who are your friends?"

"This is Nantaje, the best damned scout the army ever let get away, and this here is Mr. Louvel of the New Orleans Louvels. I call him Captain 'cause he still thinks he's fighting the war."

"A pleasure to make your acquaintance, suh. Ah understand we both fought for the correct cause."

O'Brian grinned. "You're all right, Louvel." He called over his shoulder, "You can come around. These are friends."

Ridere stepped around the corner of the cabin and stood there, the revolver hanging at his side. "This here is Harrison Ridere," O'Brian said, doing the introductions all around. "Light off those horses, gentlemen, and come out of this sun."

Chapter Eleven

"Sorry I don't have anything stronger to offer you boys than coffee, but up until a few days ago I was camping out with a plucky hellion named Ignacia who supplied all the liquor a man could drink . . . and everything else he could ask for." He winked a couple of times. "If you catch my drift." O'Brian chuckled and added, "So, tell me, John, what brings you out here?"

Keane laid out the story for O'Brian. When he had finished, O'Brian shifted upon the crate of dynamite he was sitting on and glanced at his wounded arm. "The Ortegas, you say. An Ortega done this to me just a couple days ago. I've got sort of a personal score to settle up with them on that account."

"We were planning on going to Tombstone." Ridere reminded the Irishman.

O'Brian chewed his lip, a distant look in his pale blue eyes. "I know the place you're talking about. Been there a few times myself when the mines owned it. Helped blast part of the roadway for those tracks you mentioned."

"Then you know of the trestle?" Keane asked.

"Aye, I am familiar with it."

"Think you could bring it down?"

The Irishman laughed and swept an arm at the crates of explosives stacked about. "It would be child's play . . . if I was so inclined."

"Which we are not," Ridere interjected.

Keane glanced at the younger man, eyeing the blue uniform blouse with the red chevrons of an artillery corporal on the sleeves. "What post are you off of?"

"Huachuca . . . I deserted."

"Figured as much. Tombstone is swarming with troops these days. You go there now and you'll end up behind bars."

"There are some sporting women there Harry's hankering to dally with," O'Brian noted.

Keane gave a short laugh. "Seeing those Tombstone girls can get you in big trouble, Mr. Ridere. If I was you, I'd fight shy of the border for a while, that is if you want to stay out of a military prison. There are plenty of Mexican women who would be happy to take care of you, for a price."

O'Brian said, "Dallying with Mexican women has already gotten him in trouble. An Ortega woman. Her pa was about to turn this bull into a steer. Helping him get away is how I got shot up."

"The Ortegas seem to figure prominently in all our lives here lately," Keane noted.

"Aye, that they do. There are four brothers, and they've all got sons, and hired men," O'Brian said. "It's not hard to find yourself going crosswise with at least one of 'em. And when you step on one Ortega's toes, you've got the whole family to deal with."

125

"Then I say we all have a stake in helping Nantaje free his people."

O'Brian didn't comment on that one way or the other, but Ridere said he wanted nothing to do with it.

"In that case, John Russell, there is no use mentioning the silver," Nantaje said casually.

"Silver?" O'Brian and Ridere said at once. They looked at each other, then at Nantaje. "How much silver are we talking about?" the Irishman asked.

Louvel said, "We figured about a quarter of a million, give or take a few thousand."

"Two hundred and fifty thousand dollars in silver? Ortega silver?" O'Brian's eyes were suddenly wide and eager.

"Ortega silver," Keane confirmed.

"Hm. That sorta throws a whole different light on it, don't it, Harry?"

"I don't know. . . ."

"You still thinking about Ortega's castrating knife?" Keane said.

"You saying I'm a coward?"

Keane shrugged as though he hadn't heard the challenging note in Ridere's voice. "'Course, can't say as I'd blame you much if you were."

"I'm going," Ridere said.

O'Brian looked at his bandaged arm. "The Ortegas owe me for this. You can count me in too, John."

The hacking cough drove Gaspar Ortega to his chair, and Santiago leaped from his own, rescuing his wineglass from the trembling table while the spasm held his brother helpless in its painful grasp. It lasted longer than usual.

Francisco scowled as he steadied the bottle of Madeira, concern furrowing deeply into his swarthy face. "Your cough is worsening," he noted when the ordeal had finally

126

passed. Gaspar pulled himself up straight, clutching at his chest, trying to keep the pain from showing.

"It comes and goes. Do not worry yourself about it. It is because of this news that Santiago brings. It pains me greatly. Your sons, our nephews . . . our brother, Armando . . . dead!" In spite of his weakened condition, the last word burst from his lips. His dark eyes shifted and found Santiago's unsmiling face. Santiago was the youngest of the four brothers and his complexion the fairest. He'd gotten most of their mother's Spanish blood, and her eyes, too, blue and brooding, deep-set. "The names again of the gringos responsible for it?"

"One is called Keane. I am told he was of the U.S. Army until a few years ago. The other is called Louvel. He will not be hard to recognize. Black hair and eyes, a slender man who talks with the accent of those gringos from the southern states. But more important, he has only one arm. I think he is a little *loco,* too. He lives in the past. I do not think he has ever stopped fighting the North American Civil War." Santiago's fist tightened about the crystal goblet of wine. "If only I had killed him when I had the chance!"

"You could not know, my brother," Francisco said softly. Francisco was next in line behind Gaspar, being only a year younger. He lived on a rancheria near the border with a wife whom he loved, two sons, and a daughter as wild and beautiful as a desert thunderstorm or an unbroken mustang. A daughter carrying the child of a gringo! Gaspar knew of this disgrace, although he did not know if Santiago had yet been told. It was Francisco's place to tell their younger brother.

Gaspar poured himself another glass of wine. "I promise you these men will not go unpunished. But the gringos must wait, though it stabs at my heart to do nothing right now. We have more immediate things to see to."

127

"Yes," Francisco agreed. "We must decide when we are to move the Indians to the gulf."

Gaspar produced an envelope and passed it to Francisco. "It is a telegraph from Horace. A rider brought it in this afternoon, just before you and Santiago arrived. He says the steamer *Maria* put out two days ago."

"Then it will be at Puerto Peñasco tomorrow."

"Exactly. I had hoped to have more people to ship out, but that can't be helped."

"The train will have to leave in the morning," Santiago said.

"Yes, in the morning." The hacking cough returned suddenly. The two brothers frowned at each other and waited patiently until it passed and Gaspar was once again composed. There was a knock at the door. "Come," Gaspar said.

Leandro entered and silently closed the door behind him. "Butler and his men, they will be leaving in the morning."

"Good. The man brings us much business, but he grates on my nerves."

"Then why do we not tell him to take his business elsewhere?" Santiago suggested.

Gaspar laughed. "Ah, the impetuous one you are. Just like our mother was. There is nowhere else for Butler to take his business, and besides, his business brings us much money. So long as it profits us, Santiago, I will put up with him." Gaspar smiled and turned to Leandro. "We will be shipping the Apache out in the morning. See that each gets an extra ration of food, and fill the water tanks in the cars. It is a long, hot trip to the gulf. I don't want any of the merchandise damaged before I turn it over to the captain of the *Maria*."

"I will see that it is done according to your word." Leandro left and strode down the empty street to the barracks where miners once lived when this had been a booming silver town. It was one of the few buildings still maintained and used by Ortega's men. He found the engineers playing checkers and informed them of Gaspar's orders for the next morning. They would require time to ready the locomotive for the trip to the gulf. Afterward, he looked up Hector Ramirez, who was in charge of the kitchen, and told him to prepare extra food for the captives. Finally he made his way to the holding pens and spent a few minutes watching the Apache milling about. When the wind blew just right, the odor of human feces baking under the burning Mexican sun was an assault on the nose.

"They are like caged animals, are they not?" one of the guards said, stopping alongside Leandro.

"Except that they are not animals."

"Look how the bucks pace the rail. Back and forth . . . back and forth. And see the hate that smolders in their eyes for you and me?"

"Do you blame them?"

The guard studied Leandro a moment, a thin smile on his sunburned face. "I sense in you a sympathy for these people, Leandro." He looked at the women and children, and the ever restless warriors. "No, I do not blame them. If it was me, I would try to escape. Like that buck who slipped away three nights ago. He was luckier than most, was he not, Leandro?"

Something in the man's voice made Leandro wonder how much he knew of what happened that night.

"Sympathy? They mean nothing to me," Leandro said sharply.

The guard's grin widened. "I might almost believe you, Leandro." He laughed and strolled off toward a splotch of shade beneath one of the guard towers.

Leandro left the pens and walked the length of the train, inspecting the cattle cars. There were six in all, but for this trip three would be left on the siding. There were not as many prisoners to be transported as had been the case in the past. It amazed Leandro that the mines could purchase so many people to work the deep silver pits and yet still want more. How many, he wondered, must perish beneath the ground? The thought disturbed him more than usual. He looked at his hands—hands that at one time were used to comfort, to save. And now they destroyed. When he thought of Gaspar Ortega and his brothers his fists tightened. Slowly he relaxed them and took stock of the anger he had permitted to rise dangerously close to the surface. It wasn't time—not yet, at least. But he had a feeling that it would be soon, very soon.

How long will God permit the wicked to go unpunished?

He shook the thought from his head and continued inspecting the cattle cars. Then he returned to town, gave a brief greeting to the two guards reclining near the doorway of the old vault, and made his way to the stables, where nearly fifty horses milled about. He inspected the Gatling gun Ortega had stolen from the North American army, chatted briefly with the men there, and then returned to Gaspar Ortega to report that all was in order.

The five men rode hard all that day, Nantaje in the lead, showing them the way back. O'Brian, a canvas sack hanging heavily off the side of his horse and his inside vest pockets and saddlebags bulging, had been shuffled to the rear of the column, and he was feeling particularly lonely because of the explosive cargo he was carrying. That night they made camp not far from Ortega's stronghold. With the dynamite safely stored outside camp, at everyone's insistence but O'Brian's, who couldn't understand all the fuss they were making over it, they gathered around the campfire to plan their assault.

"Ah think we should try to arrive before daylight, if that is possible," Louvel said.

"Darkness would be to our advantage," Keane agreed.

"There is more than that," Louvel went on, laying out the stronghold in the dirt with a stick. "If Nantaje has his directions accurate, the canyon opens due east. With the low morning sun in their eyes, they will be at a distinct disadvantage."

"A disadvantage that will last only half an hour at most," Keane said.

"Half an hour is all we will need to reach the town, John Russell. It lies only a few miles beyond the canyon."

Keane glanced from the ex-Confederate to the ex-scout and laughed. He looked at the two deserters sitting there and said, "What a fine company of outcasts we make. Look at us. Captain Louvel still fights a war that tore this country apart, while Corporal Ridere runs from discipline and regimentation. Nantaje here, he outlived his usefulness at what? Twenty-five? And O'Brian defected mainly because of religion." He laughed again, but there was no humor in his voice.

"And what of you, suh? What is the demon that you run from, Major Keane?"

"I already told you."

"Honor?" His eyebrows lifted slightly at the question.

"Some might call it that. Disobeying orders is what General Crook decided to call it. He gave me a choice. The army had been a good life for me, so I resigned my commission and the government sends my pension to the postmaster in Denver."

"Denver? And how long has it been since you have been back there to collect those checks, suh?"

Keane smiled. "Oh, I figure about a thousand fifty dollars ago."

Louvel laughed.

"An army pension is something I will never have to worry myself about," Ridere said.

"Nor I," O'Brian said in a growl, as if that were something he truly regretted.

"Nantaje said he saw two Gatlings and a twelve-pounder," Ridere said, coming back around to the subject at hand. "The army had similar ordnance stolen last spring. I'll bet it is the same."

"That should make it hot for us," O'Brian commented.

"Maybe, but I'm not too worried," Ridere continued. "An artillery piece like that twelve-pound field gun takes a gun crew of four cannoneers to operate it effectively. And even then we can hardly hit what we aim at. I'm thinking that if Ortega's men manage to get off one shot every five minutes, they will be doing damned good."

"What is the range on a piece like that?" Louvel asked.

"The same as it was twenty years ago when you and I were shooting them at each other, Captain," Keane replied.

"About sixteen hundred yards," Ridere said.

"What about them Gatling guns? I ain't never seen one, but hear they're murder," O'Brian said.

"There again, in the hands of a trained crew, yes. The two guns that were stolen are model 1883. Ten barrels encased in a bronze jacket, firing forty-five-caliber ammunition. In theory, a gun like that can put out anywhere from eight hundred to fifteen hundred shots per minute . . . depending on the location of the cranking lever. But there have been problems with the vertical-feed magazines, and the army has just recently gone over the new Accles feeder. But it's a complicated device and jams a lot, too. Unless Ortega's men are trained to clear the jam, it might take minutes to figure it out. In the heat of battle they will likely abandon the gun for a weapon that works every time. Then there is the fouling problem, and there is no way around that until someone invents a gunpowder that burns clean."

"You seem to know a whole bunch about them guns, Harry."

Ridere tapped the red chevron on his sleeve. "Artillery, Dougal. I did manage to learn a thing or two from the army—that is, when I wasn't cooling my heels in the guardhouse."

"Then maybe one of those Gatling guns is where you ought to be when the shooting starts, Corporal."

"I can try, Major, but I'm pretty much out of ammunition." He drew the revolver from his waistband. "I took this off a dead Mexican. I have exactly one round left."

"What caliber?"

"Forty-five."

Keane frowned. "Can't help you there. Both my guns are forty-fours. And these three are packing old cap-and-ball revolvers."

Ridere said, "Those Gatlings are forty-fives. If I can reach their ammunition boxes I'll have plenty. If I remember right, there were five thousand rounds with the guns when they were stolen."

"Don't worry, Harry," O'Brian said, reaching inside his vest. "Take a couple of these with you." He shoved two sticks of dynamite into Ridere's hand.

The young man stared at them. "I don't want these," he said, giving them back.

"Suit yourself."

"Ah thought you left all that stuff out there," Louvel said, hitching his thumb over his shoulder at the darkness beyond their fire.

"I forgot about these," the old Irishman replied. He slipped the waxed sticks back inside his canvas vest.

Keane said, "O'Brian, you can set the explosives while we make for the town. Can you manage it alone, with one good arm?"

"I think so. If I remember it right, those tracks cross that gully on an eighty-foot straining-beam truss sitting up on two bents. I'll set my charges on the stringers right in the middle where them timbers are at their largest deflection. I won't have to do no fancy monkey climbing around underneath it or anything."

"John Russell?"

Keane glanced at the Apache.

"What if my people are already gone?"

O'Brian gave a short laugh. "Then we will have wasted a lot of good dynamite for nothing."

"Reckon that's something we need to know for certain before we all go charging in there, Nantaje," Keane said. "I'll wake you in a couple hours so that you can ride ahead and scout out the town. O'Brian can show us the rest of the way there. We will await word from you at the mouth of the canyon." Keane glanced around at them. "Any other questions?"

"Just one," Louvel said. "Where is all this silver you said was there?" He looked at Nantaje.

"I do not know for certain, but one of the buildings appears to be guarded. I saw the place for a moment when I escaped." Nantaje glanced suddenly at Keane. "I forgot to tell you, John Russell. When I was making my way to the horses, one of the guards saw me. Yet he did nothing. It was almost as if he wanted me to escape."

No one spoke right away, and for a moment there was just the crackling of their fire and the far-off sounds of some quail. Keane said, "That's strange. You're sure he saw you?"

"He was as close to me as I am to you, John Russell."

Louvel looked worried. "They may be expecting us then."

"Maybe." If Ortega was expecting them, there was nothing Keane could do about that now. But being forewarned, he would be ready if that proved to be the case. "We'll have to keep our eyes open, gentlemen. But then, we already knew that. For now, I say we get some sleep."

Chapter Twelve

A few hours before dawn Nantaje slipped the hackamore over his horse's muzzle and ears and silently leaped onto its back and rode away. J. R. Keane stirred up the fire, being quiet so as not to wake the others. He put on a pot of coffee, then walked off a few hundred feet and climbed a boulder that still gave off some of yesterday's heat. He wanted to think through what was coming in the next few hours, but the desert kept intruding on his thoughts. The desert seemed to come alive after the sun went down and animals emerged to their nocturnal way of life. It was only humans, Keane mused, that lacked the good sense to stay out of the sun during the heat of the day.

When he figured enough time had passed for the coffee to be done he went back to camp and poured himself a cup.

"Nantaje get off all right?" Louvel asked, his voice low and sounding sleepy.

"About an hour ago."

The one-armed man pushed his blanket aside and went

off to take care of business. When he returned O'Brian was stirring and snorting, just coming awake. The sky was graying to the east. Keane roused O'Brian and Ridere from their blankets. No one mentioned the coming attack, as if just speaking of it might somehow put a hex on it—a chance they weren't anxious to take. They ate what they had, finished the coffee, and with the sun still below the horizon, were once again on their way.

Leandro strolled alongside the cattle cars, opening the padlock on each and hauling the heavy doors back on their iron wheels. Jakinda watched him from the holding pen. It was obvious something was up. Was today the day they were to be crowded aboard the train like so many animals and shipped off to the great waters far to the west? Almost anything would be better than the conditions they had lived in these past four or five days. But the thought of boarding that monstrous iron wagon and then being swept across the desert to a sea from which neither she, nor her son, nor any of her people would ever return was terrifying.

Every day since Nantaje had escaped, she had watched and waited for his return, but he had not come. Had he even made it out of the canyon? There had been much gunfire, and then later a company of Mexicans had ridden out in pursuit. Though they had returned empty-handed, there was no assurance her brother had not been killed, or wounded and left to die.

Now there was more activity around the black iron machine. Men were climbing upon it, busy with tasks that were beyond her comprehension. Someone had built a campfire inside the monster, and soon a thin column of smoke was rising from the chimney and men were chucking wood from the woodpile behind the monster.

"It must be today," Tejon said, the apprehension in his young voice matching her own feelings perfectly. She took him by the shoulders and pulled him to her, but the boy turned out of her grasp and stepped away. It was the warrior in him coming out now, she knew. Tejon was nearly grown, too old to be coddled by his mother, and she feared for him as only a mother could.

The food wagon came and each prisoner was given a double portion. Afterward, guards slid back the rails and the people were ordered out. Sergeant Butler and his men were there, and as each warrior filed past him, Walt Green unlocked the shackles and took them. Unencumbered by their iron bracelets and chains the Indians were herded into a cattle car. When both pens had been loaded aboard, Leandro snapped the padlocks shut. They filled three cars, packed in tight as pillow stuffing.

Jakinda watched as the soldiers saddled up, and with little ceremony, turned their horses away and left.

She gazed east, at the dark line of shadows that still clung beneath the mountains there. Hope failed her as she realized with a heavy heart that Nantaje was not coming back for them. The only thing that could have prevented him was death itself. First a husband and then a brother, gone . . . and now a son with the stirrings of a warrior's heart beginning to pound in his breast!

Moving with the sureness of a homing pigeon and the fleetness of an eagle, the Apache scout pushed the tireless pony on through the dark morning hours. Nantaje's eyes adapted to the scarcity of light as fully as any human eye could, and the horse's eyes were even more capable. Together they crossed the rugged countryside at a speed most white men would consider reckless. As dawn approached, the Indian had already found the canyon entrance where the dull twin rails led away to the distant sea. Nantaje followed them through the canyon, then cut to the north and disappeared in a series of hogbacks that folded against the mountains.

Montaña la Plata lay dark and still in the distance, almost

imperceptible except for the few scattered lights standing out like dim stars that had fallen upon the valley floor. Nantaje worked his way toward it. The rough buildings slowly emerged from shadows, dark blue at first, then graying and finally taking on a faint tinge of color. He dismounted and climbed to a ridge that overlooked the place. To his relief, the train was still there, and so were the pens crowded with his people, and another with people he did not know, but with whom he strangely felt a deep bond now.

Something caught his eye. It was the orange flicker of flames from within the dark shape of the locomotive. Where its smokestack stood above the nearby shed, a faint trace of smoke threaded skyward.

Ortega was readying the locomotive! That could mean only one thing. Today his people would be moved to the sea, and then sent far away, to another land, forever beyond hope of rescue!

Nantaje scrambled down the gravelly slope and leaped to the back of his pony. The horse sprang into a gallop at his impatient urgings, racing back to the canyon entrance where he could only hope that Keane and the others were waiting for him. If that train should leave with the bridge still standing, there would be no way for him to stop it by himself.

Ex-army Major J. R. Keane brought his small column of outcasts to a halt. Below was the railroad bridge and the ribbon of steel that entered the canyon a few hundred yards beyond. With the sun still low, most of the structure's details were lost in shadows.

"Aye, there she be," O'Brian said, "just as I remember her."

"Ah don't see the Apache," Louvel remarked, scanning the terrain, taking note of each dip and rise.

"He'll be back," Keane said.

"Let's get down there so I can start putting these charges in place."

"There he is," Ridere said, pointing to the lone rider who suddenly came from the canyon.

"They are still there, John Russell," Nantaje said when Keane met him on the roadbed. They dismounted and Ridere helped O'Brian unload the dynamite and carry it out to the middle of the bridge. Keane, Nantaje, and Louvel strode out onto it and looked down at the water rushing through the narrow defile about seventy-five feet below.

"We do not have much time, John Russell. They have put a fire in the locomotive."

"Getting up a head of steam," Keane said.

Louvel said, "Tell me of the terrain."

"This canyon opens up onto a valley. It is many miles across. The town sits on the flats, about two miles beyond. Nearby, to the left, are many ridges. Go all the way to mountains. The road from town stays on level ground, follows these tracks."

"That makes sense." Louvel thought a moment. "We can use those ridges to approach unseen."

"I'd like to see them for myself," Keane said. He looked at O'Brian. "How long will it take you to set your dynamite?"

"Give me half an hour, John . . . forty-five minutes to rig it up right and run my fuses."

"We don't have half an hour. Do you need Ridere's help, or can you manage it yourself, Dougal?"

"I can do OK alone. You take Harry with you. I'll blow this bridge, then come give you a hand. You'll know it when all this dynamite goes off. Sound carries forever in this here country."

Ridere set down the coil of fuse and went for his horse.

"Good luck, Dougal," Keane said.

"Aye, and might the saints be with the lot of you, too," O'Brian called as they started off.

"Well, Señor Ortega, it's been a pleasure doing business with you again," Sgt. Sam Butler said, grinning as he patted the sack of silver hanging from his pommel.

Gaspar Ortega nodded. "Likewise, I am sure, señor," he replied evenly, trying not to let his feelings show. Although he appreciated the business Butler brought him, Gaspar was never sad to see the man go.

Butler stepped into his stirrup and lifted himself onto the horse. "Be seeing you boys around," he said to the brothers, and turned away with his men ranging out on either side of him in no particular order as they took to the road and left Montaña la Plata behind.

Santiago and Francisco went back into town. Gaspar called Leandro to his side. "Is everything prepared?" He looked at the people crowded into the railcars.

"Yes. There is only to wait for the pressure to build in the boiler. The engineers, they say soon."

"Good, good. The water tanks?"

"I filled them myself. The Apache will have water enough to reach Puerto Peñasco."

"After that they become another man's worry. Who are you sending to guard our interests?"

"Miguel. He can be trusted."

Gaspar drew in a ragged breath. "I would go myself, but"—he tapped his chest—"This cough, it keeps me here. Perhaps next time."

Leandro grimaced, his eyes momentarily filling with compassion.

Gaspar smiled warmly. "You have a heart for the weary, for the tired, I can tell." Then he laughed. "You should have been a priest, Leandro. It would have suited you."

Leandro winced and looked away. "I will see to the final

preparations, *Patrón,"* he said, leaving the older man standing there.

Keane led the way through the canyon into the valley beyond and cut left, moving into the cover of the rocky hogbacks. Suddenly Nantaje drew rein and pointed past a break in the ridge that gave a narrow view of the road.

"There. That is Butler and his men!"

Keane grabbed the pony's rein. "Hold up, Nantaje. Where do you think you're going?"

"They are the ones who took my people, murdered Turi and the others!"

Sergeant Butler had for a brief time been under Keane's command, and if the man cared for anything or anyone, he never once showed it. Keane remembered that Butler looked out only for himself, and that was all. He had disciplined the sergeant more than once, and finally signed the transfer papers that moved him out of his company. There was no love lost between them. "I know," Keane said. "But for now we have to let him go. You take after Butler now and you will have sounded a warning for Ortega."

Nantaje's fists tightened about the reins and his jaw went rigid. Slowly he unfolded his fingers and nodded. "You are right, John Russell."

"Once your people are free and safe we can go after Butler."

They let the renegade soldiers pass.

"What about Dougal?" Ridere asked. "They are bound to spot him."

"Mr. O'Brian can take care of himself," Keane answered, but he was worried about the old Irishman, too.

"What are your plans, Major?"

Keane turned in his saddle to consider the Southerner a moment. "You're the West Point graduate, Captain. How do you make it?"

Louvel shook his head. "Suicide, suh. Sheer suicide. Apart from that, Ah say there is little profit in any sort of frontal attack. Ah say the only chance we have of accomplishing our goal is to capture the general of this army and hold him for ransom—the ransom being Nantaje's people . . . and that wagonload of silver."

"Reasonable," Keane agreed. "If we can find this man, Gaspar Ortega."

"Ortega is never alone, at least I have not seen him so," Nantaje said.

Ridere fidgeted in his saddle and looked over his shoulder. "Shouldn't we have heard something by now? Hope Dougal didn't run into trouble rigging that bridge." He watched the last of Butler's men ride past beyond the cut in the ridge. "Damn, maybe I should have stayed with him."

"Come on, we haven't got much time." They made their way as close to the town as they could without losing cover. It was open ground all the rest of the way.

"Now what?" Ridere asked.

"Perhaps a diversion," Louvel suggested.

Keane said, "What do you have in mind?"

Louvel's brow furrowed. "Ah say it is time we return their runaway to them." He looked at Nantaje.

"I'm game, John Russell."

"Game?" Ridere stared at the Apache. "Is that an Indian expression?"

Nantaje grinned. "Comes from living with the white man too long."

Louvel swung off his horse, unbuckled a saddlebag, and removed a rolled-up gray bundle. He shook it out and slipped his arm into the sleeve of the Confederate uniform blouse. "Ah shall show my true colors going into battle, suh." He looked at Keane. "Besides, if nothing else this will pique their curiosity and give you boys a chance to work your way around the back side of town. Major

Keane, will you lend me a hand with the sash? It is some-what of a challenge with only one arm."

Keane helped Louvel don the uniform, then stood back and appraised him. "You look spiffy enough to shoot, Louvel."

"You damned Yankees tried hard enough, you surely did."

"Is this your way of being unconventional?"

The Southerner grinned. "Lieutenant Colonel Custer would have likely approved. Now, if you will bind Nantaje's hands behind him, but keep the ropes lose so he can slip free of them at a moment's notice. And make sure his shirt properly hides his revolver."

"Think this will work, John Russell?" Nantaje asked as Keane put a rope about his hands.

"It had better."

Nantaje and Louvel backtracked a bit, then moved out of the broken country to the road and started for Ortega's stronghold.

"Those two, they are both crazy riding down there like that."

"Maybe. Maybe we are all just a little crazy, Corporal. Let's move out."

Dougal O'Brian quickly and expertly attached bundles of dynamite to each of the six stringers that stretched across the gulch, supporting the tracks. From the six bundles he threaded out six fuses and carefully attached them all to a single lead fuse.

"Aye, that should do her," he said, admiring his handi-work, feeling a thrill as he contemplated the explosion to come. He could visualize the center section of the bridge evaporating beneath all that explosive power. He fully expected the bridge to crumple into the raging water below. But if it still managed to remain standing, the weight of the next train to use it would do the trick. A worried look suddenly scrunched his face. If that next train happened to be carrying all those Apache . . .

He considered the structure again, wondering if he shouldn't put a couple more charges on the overhead trusses just to make sure the whole thing did end up in a pile at the bottom of the ravine. Then he heard a sharp crack sing through the rails. He glanced at the canyon mouth where the tracks disappeared and went to his knees and put an ear to one of them. There it was again, a sharp ringing, as if someone had struck it with a hammer . . . or an iron horseshoe! It was too soon for Keane and the others to be coming back, but someone was surely coming.

O'Brian quickly fished a brass match safe from his pocket, withdrew a lucifer, and struck fire to it. He set the long lead fuse to spitting sparks and curling smoke, and hurried off the bridge to where his horse waited.

"Let's get outta sight, girl," he said, taking up the reins and looking around to make sure he'd left nothing behind—nothing except a burning fuse and fifty pounds of dynamite. He led the horse down a slope and into some rocks that hid it from view. He drew his revolver and moved across the rocky slope to a place where he could watch both the bridge and the mouth of the canyon.

In the rush to get under cover he'd lost track of the minutes. His view shifted between the burning fuse and the canyon. He was still too close and knew it would be safer to move off a couple hundred yards. Then he saw the soldiers. Nantaje had said that the men who had captured his people had been renegade soldiers from Fort Bowie. The men had drawn rein and were surveying the land beyond the canyon. He could hear their horses snorting and pawing the hard roadbed.

One of them said, "I sure can use a drink, Sam. Which way do you make it to the nearest cantina?"

"In this hellhole? Probably Fronteras."

"Then that's where I want to go. We got money in our pockets, and whiskey and girls are a good way to spend some of it."

"Yeah, and in a week you will be broke again," another put in. "I'm for taking my cut and heading down to Mexico City."

"I'm with Hennigan. When we gonna split up the money, Sam?"

"We split it when I say so."

"That ain't fair, Sam. We all took the risks; I think we ought to have our share of the silver right now."

"Hey, Sam? What's that out yonder?" one of the renegades asked, pointing. They stopped their arguing and studied the trail of smoke.

"Looks like something's afire," someone said.

"Smells like sulfur to me," a thickset soldier said, sniffing the air.

"Let's take a look." The leader rode out onto the bridge and stared an instant at the sputtering cord.

"Damn!" O'Brian cussed under his breath, sidling along the rock to a place where he could better watch them.

"That there is dynamite fuse, Sam!"

The leader glanced from the center of the bridge, then back to the canyon they had just emerged from. "What the hell is going on here? Green, kill that fuse!"

One of the men jumped out of his saddle.

"Damnation!" O'Brian growled. "Always somebody wanting to ruin the party." He drew a bead on the man. It was a long shot for a revolver and he caught his breath just before squeezing the trigger. The gun barked and Green lurched two steps to one side and fell over the side of the bridge.

The men were in motion. O'Brian fired again as they wheeled their horses around, drawing their weapons at the same time. He sent a third shot that went wide. It was

145

returned by a volley of bullets that drove him back behind the rock.

He glanced around it to see their horses scrambling for the end of the bridge; then there was a flash of blinding light and a roar like a hundred Niagras. The concussion slammed O'Brian to the ground, stunned, and the next instant the air was sucked from his lungs and an elephant stepped down hard on his chest. His vision blurred as he lay there helpless and bits and pieces of timber began raining down on him.

Chapter Thirteen

"Hope you know what you are doing," Nantaje said when the four Mexicans came from the old warehouse at the edge of town.

"Let me do the talking."

Nantaje tilted his chin up at the open double door on the second floor. "Gatling gun up there."

"Noted."

The Mexicans ranged out around them, rifles in hand. They only glanced at the Apache; their attention was drawn to the one-armed man in the Confederate officer's uniform. "Señor, who are you? What do you want here?"

"My name is Capt. Royden Louvel. Ah am looking for a man called Gaspar Ortega. Ah believe Ah have something that belongs to him."

They looked again at the Apache. "This is the one who escaped."

"He showed up at my campfire two nights ago. Ah fed him and listened to his story. His English is quite good, learned while a scout for the United States Army. Ah have a particular dislike for that army, as you might well imagine, since Ah see you have noted my uniform. After he told me of this place Ah captured the rascal." Louvel grinned. "Ah'm not a rich man and Ah was hoping Mr. Ortega would look kindly on my returning the runaway to him."

A Mexican wearing a scarlet shirt said, "Hernando, report this to Ortega."

"Yes." The man hurried back into town.

Louvel squinted at the morning sun and said, "It grows hot. Do you mind if I wait in the shade of that building?"

"You may."

Word of their arrival spread, and soon three other men stood there. Nantaje continued peering straight ahead. Louvel merely smiled at them and looked around.

They all heard the distant rumble. One of the Mexicans thought it was thunder. Nantaje caught Louvel's eye and gave a small nod. Only they understood the true nature of the boom.

A steam whistle blared and a plume of black smoke billowed over the rooftops to Nantaje's left. He cast a worried look at Louvel, but there was nothing the Southerner could do just then except hitch his shoulders in a barely perceptible shrug.

"Who are you?" a man who had appeared around the corner of the building asked.

"My name is Captain Louvel, C.S.A."

"C.S.A.? Bah! Are you *loco,* man? The Confederate states lost their war twenty years ago. What is it you want from me?"

Louvel stiffened. "Ah prefer to think of it as a temporary setback, suh. We are merely regrouping. The South shall rise again—but that is another matter. Ah have brought your Apache back." He hesitated. "Ah thought there might be something in it for me."

"Something? You speak of money?"

"What else is there, Mr. Ortega?"

Gaspar laughed and looked at Nantaje. "We did have one escape." He stifled a cough. "Where did you find him?"

"Showed up in my camp looking hungry and tired. Since he appeared to be docile for a redskin, Ah fed him, then captured him."

"Hm. Yes, I can give you something for his return."

Louvel smiled as if he was pleased.

"Take the Indian away and put him aboard the train with the others."

One of Ortega's men took the reins to Nantaje's pony. "Leandro has the key," he said.

"Then find Leandro! Come with me, Señor Louvel."

He stepped down off his horse. The train's whistle sounded again, followed by a rush of steam, then another. Black smoke erupted skyward and the locomotive began to crawl forward.

Gaspar frowned as the train started moving.

"It is too late," the one holding Nantaje's horse said.

Fighting down a momentary panic, Nantaje forced himself to think calmly as the cattle cars crept slowly past and the engine picked up speed. The train had to be stopped before it reached the gulch. He could easily catch it now, if he could get away. But with so many guns, that was impossible.

"What is it?" This was the voice of a newcomer.

Nantaje turned and their eyes met. He knew this man. He was the one who had allowed him to escape. The man had gone rigid, too, recognizing Nantaje.

"Ah, Leandro. This is that Apache who escaped," Gaspar said as the train had moved off in a black cloud and a fine shower of ash fell gently upon them. "See that he is put under lock and key. He will not be so lucky this time."

"Yes, *Patrón.*"

Louvel said, "Ah perceive that this redskin was intended to be upon that train, Mr. Ortega?"

"He was. It cannot be helped now." Gaspar watched the train shrinking in the distance. "But there will be other trains. Come with me." They started into town.

Just then Santiago and Francisco stepped from a building. Louvel sucked in a startled gasp and felt his heart pounding. He hadn't expected to find them here.

The two brothers started across the street to meet them. All at once Santiago stopped. His face turned hard with a scowl settling deeply upon it. "You!" he said with a growl, grabbing his gun from the holster.

"What is it?" Gaspar asked.

Santiago rushed forward, his knuckles blanching around the grip of his Colt. "This one, he was with Keane! He is the one who warned him. He more than anyone else is responsible for the death of Armando, our nephews . . . my son! You! You with your false friendship and lying tongue! I will silence that tongue now!" Santiago thumbed the hammer of his revolver and put the gun to Louvel's head.

Louvel laughed at him. "Suh, where is retribution in merely blowing out my brains? Is there satisfaction in so instant an execution? Where is the honor? You are correct. Ah did warn Keane of your plans. Honor dictated that Ah should. If it is revenge you seek, then do so in a manly manner . . . with honor! Ah challenge you to use your fists, suh, or does the thought of fighting a one-armed man frighten you?"

"Frightened? Me? Of you?" Santiago shoved the gun into the holster. "I will delight in watching you squirm upon the street, begging for mercy, señor, pleading that I should kill you—and kill you I will, but *muy* slowly." He passed the gun belt to Francisco and curled his fists.

"You will permit me to remove my coat? Ah wouldn't want it soiled." Louvel untied the sash and worked the buttons, laying the garments off to one side. One of Gaspar's men took his gun belt. The Southerner hunched low and the two men circled as more of Ortega's men drifted out of buildings to watch.

From his place alongside the warehouse, Nantaje noted the men gathering to watch the fight. All that remained at their posts were the two guards in front of one building, and those men on either end of town manning the Gatling guns. But everyone's attention was on the two men circling in the street. If he was ever going to make his break, Nantaje knew the time was now.

Leandro said, "Why did you come back?"

"To free my people." Nantaje slipped his hands from the loose ropes. He could overpower this man now, but Leandro had let him go once. Perhaps he would do so again. "I must stop that train," he said urgently.

"Yes, I know. Once it reaches the gulf, your people will never return."

"No, you do not know. It is more urgent than that," Nantaje said. "The bridge is gone. If the train is not stopped, my people will all be killed."

"The bridge?" Leandro glanced around suspiciously and lowered his voice. "You must go quickly, my son."

Nantaje handed him the rope.

Leandro looked at it, then managed a small smile. "You two, you are in this together?"

"Yes. And there are more. I do not know why you are helping me, señor, but now I will help you. Find someplace to hide, and do not come out until it is all over."

"Until what is all over?"

Nantaje reined his horse around.

"Wait." The Mexican reached into a pocket for a key. "Here. You will need this to open the locks."

Nantaje took it from him.

"Go with God, my son," Leandro said as the Apache slipped away unnoticed and heeled his horse into motion.

* * *

151

Circling, Louvel tracked Santiago with the eye of a panther, reading every movement, every blink, every muscle twitch. Having only one arm put him at a great disadvantage, but twenty years of drifting from town to town, taking whatever life threw at him and turning it around and throwing it back, had trained him well. His body had adjusted. His reflexes had become just a bit quicker, his aim surer, his muscles stronger, and his nerves had developed the temper of fine steel drawn file-hard in the fires of life.

Santiago shot a jab at Louvel's gut. Louvel danced easily aside and clipped the Mexican on the chin. They circled again. Louvel saw it coming and ducked under Santiago's fist. He drove up hard under the Mexican's ribs and folded him in half.

Kneeling in the dirt and clutching his stomach, Santiago glared up at him, the hate in his blue eyes ten times hotter than the flames of hell.

"Ah wonder who squirms upon the road now," Louvel taunted, crouched, his left arm slowly windmilling.

Santiago sprang with surprising speed and plunged like a bull in the ring. Louvel barely turned aside in time, yet Santiago managed to grab his shirt and wrench him around as he charged past. Louvel staggered into the arms of one of the watchers. Someone stretched out a foot. They pushed him back at Santiago and he sprawled headlong into the street, barely able to break his fall.

Santiago leaped atop Louvel and the two men rolled into the legs of some of the onlookers. In spite of his strength, the Southerner couldn't free himself from the Mexican's grasp. He'd lost the advantage of speed, and now Santiago had the upper hand. They grappled in the dust until Santiago managed to lever Louvel's arm up behind his shoulder blades. With his other hand grabbed a hank of hair and yanked his head back.

"You want to see who is to squirm, señor? Now I will

show you!" Santiago trapped Louvel's wrist beneath his knee and slipped his knife from its sheath. Breathing hard, he said with a growl, "Have you ever seen a man's scalp taken?"

Louvel bowed his back, but Santiago's weight was too much for him. The effort only pulled harder at his arm until every muscle and every tendon cried out.

"Ah have seen men who have lost an arm carrying it across a bloody battlefield, as if somehow they imagine they might rescue it. Ah have seen soldiers with their guts spilled across the filthy ground, trying to stuff them back inside. Ah have seem men charge into the face of cannon fire for God and country! Ah don't think Ah have missed much by being denied the dubious honor of seeing a scalping, suh!"

"I was right. You are *loco!*"

Louvel strained against his weight.

"You will be denied that honor no longer." Santiago put the blade to Louvel's hairline.

Suddenly the *rat-tat-tat* of a Gatling gun ripped through the town, stitching a deadly seam down the middle of the street. Men screamed and fell while others dashed for cover. Startled, Santiago glanced up. At the same instant Louvel bowed his back and bucked the man off. A cloud of gunsmoke billowed from the stables at the edge of town as bullets threw up clouds of dust on the street behind the fleeing men. Three or four men dove into the building where the guards had been. Others fled down alleys.

Louvel scrambled to his feet. He was a moment faster than Santiago and struck out with the toe of his boot, catching the Mexican in the jaw. Santiago lurched backward. Santiago hit the ground, rolled, and jumped to his feet, the knife still in his fist.

The roar of the Gatling gun filled the town, and windows seemed to be shattering everywhere. In a glance, Louvel saw wounded men lying about. Those who weren't had made themselves scarce and now it was just he and Santiago.

From the warehouse the second Gatling began to chatter, only to fall silent after a few moments. But the one at the far end of town kept pouring lead into the town, its barrels now directed at the warehouse, where the wooden walls seemed to disintegrate before Louvel's eyes.

Suddenly it went silent, too. From one of the buildings return fire began chipping away at the livery. Louvel wondered what had happened to Ridere, and Nantaje and Keane, too. But he had no time to think about that. The blade in Santiago's fist glinted in the sunlight as the Mexican lunged.

Hurrying down a weedy alley, John Keane caught glimpses of the main street and men diving for cover. Some just lit out for the hills, and he let them go. It was the men who stayed who worried him. The rapid fire of the Gatling gun chewed through the dry buildings, leaving few places for men to hide.

Then the gun went silent. Keane figured Ridere was just reloading, but when it remained quiet, he backtracked and slipped into the cavernous building. At first it appeared abandoned, but then he heard sounds coming from the hayloft overhead. He shoved his revolver back in his holster, grabbed a rung of the ladder nailed to the wall, and hurried up it. Mounting the loft, Keane spied the Gatling gun facing the open doors out onto the street. Beyond it he could see Louvel and Santiago stalking each other like two tigers looking for an opening to pounce.

But no Ridere. Then he heard sounds from beyond a wall where a door hung half-open. Keane drew his gun and kicked the door back. Two Mexicans were trying to move some big wooden crates. They spun around when he burst through, reaching for their guns.

Keane fanned the hammer, muzzle blasting, barrel leaping, until the hammer snapped on a spent cartridge. As the roar of gunfire left Keane's ears and the smoke cleared, Ridere struggled out from behind one of the crates.

"Damn glad to see you, Keane!"

"What is this about?"

Ridere looked at one of the dead men. "Francisco Ortega. He was bound and determined, that one." The young man was shaken. "Too close." He drew in a ragged breath. "That's the second time one of you guys has hauled my fat out of the fire."

"Get that Gatling gun back in action!"

Ridere jumped to the gun and lifted the doughnut-shaped Accles feeder off the top of it. "I was trying to reload when they jumped me," he said, exchanging it for a fully loaded one.

Bullets sprayed the livery from half a dozen different directions, splintering the flimsy boards. There was no telling where the next one would come from. "Over there. That building across the way." Keane pointed at a place where the gunfire was heaviest.

Ridere tried for it but the gun's flexible yoke did not allow for enough elevation. "Can't get to them, J. R.!" Ridere suddenly pointed and said, "Look!"

In the street, Louvel and Santiago were locked in a death match. Louvel fell beneath the Mexican, his single hand desperately trying to keep the knife from his throat.

Keane dove back through the doorway and grabbed a Winchester from one of the dead Mexicans. With wood splintering all around him, he propped the rifle on his fist atop one of the Gatling gun's carriage wheels, steadied its sights, and fired.

Santiago lurched off Louvel. The Southerner scrambled to his feet and dashed for the cover of one of the buildings as bullets kicked up puffs of dust at his heels.

"Nice shot," Ridere said, spinning the crank and spraying the town. He still couldn't reach the upper level of the building where most of the return fire was coming from.

"I'll take care of them," Keane shouted above the chatter of the gun.

He hurried down the ladder and out the side door. Sprinting along the rear of the buildings through knee-high weeds, he wondered just how he could silence those guns. He came to a side street and was about to dash across it when he spied the answer to his dilemma.

The twelve-pounder was unloaded, and it was facing the wrong direction. Keane grabbed one of the tall wheels and put all his strength behind it. It barely budged. He strained again, the heel of the big gun dragging a few inches farther before stopping.

A pistol fired nearby and a bullet careened off the cannon's bronze barrel. Keane dropped to the ground and grabbed for his revolver.

Two Mexicans came out the back door of the building across the street, guns blazing. Keane snapped off a shot and flattened behind the carriage tongue as a bullet took a chip from one of the spokes; two more slammed into the heavy oak carriage. Suddenly another gun spoke, muffled by the walls of the building, and the Mexicans reeled into the street. A moment later a man appeared in the doorway gripping a revolver. He looked down at the bodies, then across at Keane, then holstered the revolver and strode toward the cannon.

Keane had him square in his sights, but there was no fear in the man's eyes, only a deep sadness. He glanced at the revolver and said, "I will help you with the big gun, señor. Do you know how to work it?"

"I do." Then he understood. "You're the one who let Nantaje escape."

"The Apache? Is that his name?"

"That's the name." Keane grabbed one of the big

wheels; the stranger took the other. Working together they got the two-thousand-pound gun turned and facing the building across the street.

Keane flung open the cartridge box on the caisson, grabbed out two wool cartridge bags, and slid them down the barrel. He pushed them into the bore with the rammer, then slammed the rod hard, compacting them.

"There should be a friction tube in that forward compartment," Keane said, hefting a heavy shell from the ammunition box. The Mexican found the device while Keane shoved the shell into the bore and rammed it against the powder charges. He located the priming wire and drove it hard through the vent hole, puncturing the cartridge bags. Sighting along the barrel, Keane made final adjustments in elevation, then inserted the friction tube into the vent hole and threaded the lanyard through the loop.

"Stand clear!"

Keane gave the lanyard a sharp yank. The cannon roared and bucked and rolled back half a dozen feet on its unchocked wheels. Across the way a corner of the building disintegrated into a thousand flying pieces of kindling. It sagged on one side, hung there briefly as timbers snapped and groaned, then slowly collapsed in on itself. A few men leaped out windows like rats escaping a sinking ship, and that was all. The gunfire ceased and the air grew strangely quiet. The silence was sharpened by the occasional burst from Ridere's Gatling gun as he chased down the few fleeing men left.

Keane leaned upon the caisson as the cloud of cannon smoke slowly dissipated in the hot air. Then he glanced at the Mexican. "Thanks for your help. But I don't understand. Why did you do it?"

The man thought a moment. "Three years ago the Ortegas attacked my village. They took many of my people, stole what little silver and gold there was, and ravaged our church, finally burning it to the ground. I vowed then to destroy the Ortegas' family of crime and to return what they had stolen. Unfortunately, I can never return the people. But the silver and gold they took from our church, this I can return. I joined with them because it was the only way. I became trusted, all the while searching for their weak spot."

"It that why you let Nantaje go?"

"No. I let the Indian escape because it was not in my heart to stop him. I did not know that doing so would be the means God used to bring down the Ortegas. Not until he returned with you and the others."

Louvel came around the corner just then, a rifle hitched under his arm. He drew up warily when he spied Keane and the Mexican. Keane motioned him over. "So who are you?"

"My name is Leandro Menendez. Father Leandro Menendez."

"You're a priest?"

"I am, although for these years I have not led the life of a priest. I have much to make amends for, but at least now our people will no longer need to fear the Ortegas."

Louvel looked at the shattered building across the way, at the smoke and dust drifting out across the town, then at Keane. "Ah see you and Ridere made it in the back door all right."

"It was wide open for us, thanks to you and Nantaje. This is Father Leandro Menendez. He's the one who helped Nantaje, and he gave me a hand when I needed it, too."

"A man of the cloth?"

"*Sí*, a man of the cloth with much repenting to do. I will spend many hours on my knees, I fear."

Keane looked around, suddenly concerned. "Where is Nantaje?"

"Ah haven't seen him," Louvel said.

"The Apache?" Leandro inquired. "He went that way." The priest pointed to the smudge of smoke in the distance.

"The train," Louvel said.

They looked at each other, and as if each read the other's mind said, "The bridge!"

Chapter Fourteen

Nantaje rode like the wind, the stout pony beneath him giving all he demanded and more. It was as if the animal knew what Nantaje knew—that if the train did not stop before reaching the bridge, everyone would be lost. He thought of Jakinda, and of Tejon, then forced them out of his brain. He could afford to concentrate on only one goal, and that was reaching the train in time.

Already the swaying cattle cars had grown larger. Slowly he was gaining on them. Nantaje dug his heels harder as he laid low to cut the wind. Five more minutes brought him up even with the last car, its cargo of people, their faces pressed to the sides, watching as the iron rungs of a ladder came within his reach. He grabbed hold of it and swung off the horse, clinging there while the great swaying beast tried to buck him off. The roar of the engine, its pumping pistons, its hissing steam, made him remember stories told to him as a child about the old times, when mountain demons lived and roamed the land.

Bracing himself against this onslaught to his senses, Nantaje pulled himself up the iron rungs and dragged himself onto the top of the cattle car. Below, faces watched him, but he did not see Jakinda or Tejon. There was a catwalk along the top of the car. He mounted it and hurried forward beneath a shower of fine ash.

The catwalk ended. He stared down at the ties flashing past below and panic rose in his breast as he realized what he had to do. He backed up a few steps, made a running leap, and crashed down on hands and knees. That wasn't so bad, he decided as he steadied himself and sprinted along the second car, this time not breaking stride but making a flying leap to the next car. His landing was much improved, and Nantaje hurried forward to the engine tender that was filled with firewood. Beyond the tender growled the puffing monster itself, its fiery belly exposed to the men who fed it constantly to satisfy its voracious appetite.

Nantaje sprawled on the catwalk so as not to be seen while he debated how to make them stop this mechanical monstrosity. His eyes found another iron ladder and he crawled to it and climbed down the side of the car. Beyond the slats he spied Jakinda forcing her way through the crowd. She grabbed his hand. He gave it a squeeze, then pulled free.

As he hung off the side of the cattle car a few feet above the clattering wheels, a long stretch put his fingers within reach of a bar running the length of the tender. He curled his hand around it and swung out, grabbing with his other hand, hanging there, working his way to the front of the tender. He stepped up on a narrow iron lip, clutched a handhold with one hand, drew his revolver with the other, and turned inside the cab of the locomotive.

"No one move!" he ordered in Spanish, swinging the Colt to cover all three men there at once.

The engineer froze with his hand upon the throttle. The other man had just grabbed up a length of wood. The

Mexican guard was eating tamales from a plate balanced on his knees. Startled by Nantaje's unexpected appearance he stood, and the tin plate clattered to the iron floor.

The one at the tender pitched the log at Nantaje.

He ducked and fired. The engineer grabbed a huge monkey wrench and swung it, striking the iron door frame above his head. Nantaje's second bullet slammed him in the chest, kicking him out the other side of the cab. By this time the guard was reaching for his revolver. Nantaje put a bullet through the man's shoulder and the guard hit the floor and banged his head upon a hissing steam valve.

Nantaje pulled himself the rest of the way into the cab and his eyes leaped along the confusion of levers and chains and valves there. He stared at the moving needles behind their glass windows. None of it made any sense to him. He touched a lever. It was hot. He gave it a shove. Nothing happened. The smell of hot oil stung his nose and brought tears to his eyes. He tugged a chain overhead and leaped back when the steam whistled its defiant protest. Reluctantly, he admitted that he could fiddle with this white man's contraption all day and never figure out how to strike a death blow to it.

Out the forward window the rocky ledges of the canyon loomed just ahead. He had no time to waste. With a final glance at the unfathomable controls, Nantaje jumped onto the tender and scrambled up the woodpile. He dug out the key Leandro had given him, clenched it in his teeth, and sprang out, catching one of the slats. The impact stunned him, and it took all his strength just to hold on as he slowly slid down until his feet touched the edge of the car. He tried not to look at the ground passing beneath him, but inched along the side of the car to the sliding door.

The first padlock opened and the door slid back and slammed against its stops, nearly jolting him off. He hardly noticed over the roar of the engine and the pull of the wind in his hair.

"Out! Quickly! All of you!" Leaping from this swaying car would be terrifying, but the only other choice was instant death at the bottom of the ravine. "Quickly! The bridge is gone and you will all die if you do not jump now!"

Nantaje had done all that he could and now it was up to them. He worked his way along the car to the end, turned the corner, and sprang for the second car. He was getting the hang of it even though his hands were bleeding from the slivers he'd taken. The second padlock snapped open, and momentum carried the door back. Once again he gave his warning.

A shadow swept over him when the train had entered the canyon. "Quickly! There is no time to waste!"

The final car was in his reach. He jumped. His foot missed the ledge and his legs swung down near the rumbling wheels. Grappling at the rough wood, he felt pain stab down his arm as his muscles strained. Nantaje groped with his free hand, caught the cold iron of a ladder rung, and slowly heaved himself up until his feet found purchase. He stood there a moment breathing hard, arms folded through the slats.

He saw the slash of daylight ahead, the canyon's mouth widening as if to spit them out—spit them into the oblivion of the ravine beyond. Nantaje drew on whatever reserves he had left and made his way once again toward the padlock.

Anxious faces awaited him, for word had already reached them that the bridge was out and instant death lay just beyond this canyon. Nantaje grabbed the key from his teeth and stuck it in the lock. The car lurched sideways in a hard curve. He reeled and stabbed at the slats to break his fall. In the effort the key flew from his fingers. He reached and missed, and saw it bounce once on the gravel and disappear.

Hanging there, Nantaje saw the end of the canyon

approach. He glanced at the padlock and panic squeezed his chest. He drove it back, turning to the frightened faces looking out at him.

"You!" he shouted, reaching through the slats for one of the women and grabbing her by the arm. Startled, she tried to pull away. He stuck his arm through and snatched the wooden hairpin from her long, black tresses.

Nantaje forced all other thoughts from his head. What he had to do, he had to do swiftly or they were all going to die. He stuck the pin into the keyhole, shut his eyes, and worked it as he'd been taught by the Fort Bowie jailers. His fingers must be his eyes now. They alone would allow him to see the tumblers move and line up "like little trooper boys," the soldiers used to say.

He stopped counting the seconds. He could permit nothing to intrude upon his concentration. One tumbler clicked, then a second, and finally the last one fell into place. He gave a tug. The lock snapped open and the door slammed back. The Apache leaped out, hitting the rocky ground hard and rolling away from the rushing wheels.

Then the canyon walls fell away, and burning sun stabbed his eyes a moment before the train reached the sagging bridge with its twisted rails. The locomotive plunged over the precipice, smoke trailing from its stack all the way down to the cold waters below. Then the boiler exploded and a deadly cloud of scalding steam screamed out of the ravine. . . .

They collected the bodies and laid them out in the shade of a building.

"That's all of 'em," Ridere said, peering down at the row of corpses.

Leandro stood over each one of them and said a prayer for their souls. Afterward, he told Keane eight men were missing, including Gaspar Ortega.

"Ah saw some men flee into the hills," Louvel said, staring at the bodies with the despair of a man who had seen death before—lots of it. Keane had seen death, too, but a man never got used to the sight. And that was a good thing. Keane pitied a people for whom violent death was not a disturbing event.

Ridere turned away and peered up the shattered building that Keane's cannon shot had left behind. "You say Ortega's gold and silver are in there?"

Leandro looked over. "He kept it in the old vault."

"Looks like we got us some digging to do, then."

"It belongs to the people of Sonoyta," Leandro said. "And to the church."

Ridere laughed. "We'll see about that, *Padre.*"

Keane said, "I'm worried about Nantaje and O'Brian."

Louvel peered at the distant mountains. "They should be back here by now."

"I almost forgot about them." Ridere temporarily put aside the problem of getting at all the loot. "I'm going to go look for them."

"I'll ride with you," Keane said.

"Ah'll go along, too."

They collected their horses and started out of town. "You don't think those renegades got Dougal?" Ridere said worriedly.

Keane didn't reply, but he was worried, too. Then Louvel drew to a halt and stood in his stirrups. "Over there. Do you see that?"

Keane strained to see into the hazy distance. "It's them. It has got to be." They kicked their horses into motion, and soon the column of people came sharply into view.

Limping, Nantaje stopped. He was holding the reins to O'Brian's horse, with the old Irishman in the saddle, clutching the horn and looking dazed. There was a woman beside him, and a boy. Behind them were the Apache, some walking under their own power, others being helped along.

"Well, well, will you look at that. The Pied Piper of Montaña la Plata!"

"John Russell. It is good to see you alive."

Keane laughed. "And I might say the same." He looked at the line of Apache, then at the Irishman. "What happened to you, O'Brian?"

O'Brian squinted as if trying to bring Keane into focus. "I reckon I overdone it a mite on that dynamite, John," he said, swaying slightly in the saddle.

"I found him under a pile of timber, John Russell. Thought he was dead at first. What happened in town?"

"Town is secure. Some of Ortega's men got away, but most won't be going anywhere but to the bottom of a six-foot hole. Looks like you managed to save your people."

"There are many who are hurt."

"Let's get them into town and see what we can do for them."

Nantaje scrambled over the twisted iron and hauled himself to the roof of the crumpled cab. He leaped to a rock rising from the rushing water and clawed his way up the side of the deep ravine. Keane gave him a hand up the final couple of feet. "I found three of them, John Russell," he said, puffing from the climb. "They are beyond recognition. O'Brian's dynamite made a big mess of them. And the crows and coyotes took care of what was left."

"You don't know if Butler is one of them?"

The Apache shook his head. The wind shifted. He wrinkled his nose and they distanced themselves from a bloated horse lying nearby. "He might have made it out, or he might be buried under that train. Maybe we will never know."

"Maybe it is best we just assume he is buried, Nantaje. You have better things to do than to try tracking someone who might be dead." Keane nodded at the Apache waiting on the road. Most were mounted on horseback now, and a few carried rifles and revolvers taken from the dead Mexicans. "Besides, they need you now."

Nantaje nodded. "For a while, until they find someplace to make a new home."

The two men returned to where the others waited, and reported what they had found.

O'Brian said, "They were on the bridge when it blew. Can't imagine anyone surviving that explosion."

Keane swung up onto his saddle. Feeling the thick sack of silver coins that rubbed against his thigh made him glance at Father Leandro sitting upon the wagon seat, holding a fistful of reins. A tarp was stretched over the silver that filled the back of the freighter. Keane looked at Ridere and O'Brian and said, "Guess this is where we part company."

"Reckon so, John."

"Got any idea where you are heading?"

"Aye. Harry and me, we figure on accompanying the good Father as far as Sonoyta."

"Just to make sure he doesn't lose all that silver," Ridere put in, sounding disappointed that all he got out of it was a single sack of coins. But even in that, it was more money than he'd ever seen in one place. And it was all his. Father Leandro had insisted all he wanted was what the Ortegas had stolen, and some extra to rebuild his church. The rest, he said, was their just reward for helping him get the stolen treasure back.

O'Brian scratched at the scar beneath his beard and said, "Afterward, I think me and Harry will just head on over to California. Hear there is a real quiet little farming village near the ocean where the señoritas are feisty and the tequila is plentiful."

"Yeah," Ridere said. "Real feisty!"

Louvel laughed. "You be careful around those belles, Mr. Ridere. You know what almost happened to you the last time."

"I'll be extra careful this time, Mr. Louvel."

"You ever need another bridge blown up, John, you just look me up."

"I will. What's the name of this sleepy little village you're heading to?"

"It's called *El Pueblo de Nuestra Señora la Reina de Los Angeles de Poricuncula*. Los Angeles, for short."

Louvel, Nantaje, and Keane watched Father Leandro and the wagon of silver rumble away with Ridere and O'Brian on either side.

"I go, too, John Russell. We need to find a place to make our village, somewhere far away from the white soldiers and the wars." He patted the sack of silver hanging off the pony's withers. "But now we have this to trade for the things we will need."

"I hope you find what you're looking for, Nantaje."

"Where are you heading, John Russell?"

The ex-army major shrugged his wide shoulders and shook his head. "Don't know where I will end up, Nantaje. But I have got some reward money waiting for me in Tombstone; then I think I'll head up to Denver City and make a deposit, along with all those army pension checks the postmaster has been collecting for me. After that, who knows?"

Nantaje extended his hand. "Thank you again, John Russell."

"You and your people take care."

Nantaje and Gato started the Apache into the desert.

Keane glanced at the Southerner. "Well, Captain Louvel, looks like it's just you and me."

"Looks that way, Major."

"Reckon you'll be heading out to Santa Cruz."

"Ah might do that, suh."

"Or you might accompany me to Denver City."

Louvel looked at him, then nodded. "And Ah might do that, too. Ah have never been to Denver City. Ah'm certain there would be a lively card game somewhere in a place like that. Got me a stake now." He touched the sack of coins tied to his saddle horn. "I could put this to good use in Denver City."

"You could deposit it, too."

"In a damned Yankee bank? Not on your life, suh!"

Keane laughed and clucked his horse ahead. Louvel fell in alongside him.

"Aren't we a pair, Major?"

"A butternut and a billy Yank?"

"Ah must be getting old. Never thought Ah'd live to see the day Ah'd saddle partner with a damned Yankee."

"Stranger things have happened."

"Not in this lifetime, Ah assure you."

THE GALLOWSMAN

WILL CADE

Ben Woolard is a man ready to start over. The life he's leaving behind is filled with ghosts and pain. He lost his wife and children, and his career as a Union spy during the war still doesn't sit quite right with him, even if the man sent to the gallows by his testimony was a murderer. But now Ben's finally sobered up, moved west to Colorado, and put the past behind him. But sometimes the past just won't stay buried. And, as Ben learns when folks start telling him that the man he saw hanged is alive and in town—sometimes those ghosts come back.

___4452-8 $4.50 US/$5.50 CAN

CHEYENNE

DOUBLE EDITION
JUDD COLE

One man's heroic search for a world he can call his own.

Arrow Keeper. A Cheyenne raised among pioneers, Matthew Hanchon has never known anything but distrust. The settlers brand him a savage, and when Matthew realizes that his adopted parents will suffer for his sake, he flees into the wilderness—where he'll need a warrior's courage if he hopes to survive.

And in the same volume...

Death Chant. When Matthew returns to the Cheyenne, he doesn't find the acceptance he seeks. The Cheyenne can't fully trust any who were raised in the ways of the white man. Forced to prove his loyalty, Matthew faces the greatest challenge he has ever known.

___4280-0 $4.99 US/$5.99 CAN

CHEYENNE

Double Edition:
Pathfinder/ Buffalo Hiders
JUDD COLE

Pathfinder. Touch the Sky never forgot the kindness of the settlers, and tried to help them whenever possible. But an old friend's request to negotiate a treaty between the Cheyenne and gold miners brings the young brave face-to-face with a cunning warrior. If Touch the Sky can't defeat his new enemy, the territory will never again be safe for pioneers. *And in the same action-packed volume...*

Buffalo Hiders. Once, mighty herds of buffalo provided the Cheyenne with food, clothing and skins for shelter. Then the white hunters appeared and the slaughter began. Still, few herds remain, and Touch the Sky swears he will protect them. But two hundred veteran mountain men and Indian killers are bent on wiping out the remaining buffalo—and anyone who stands in their way.

___4413-7 $4.99 US/$5.99 CAN

SUNDANCE

HANGMAN'S KNOT/APACHE WAR

PETER McCURTIN

Hangman's Knot. Sundance doesn't think twice about shooting the drunken coward in a saloon brawl. But Judge Isaac Parker, the infamous Hanging Judge, thinks differently. Sundance receives an instant death sentence, but if he captures the feared half-breed outlaw Joe Buck, he will be freed. There is only one problem: Buck is Sundance's old trail partner.

And in the same action-packed volume . . .

Apache War. Sundance is dispatched on a mission to Fort McHenry, Arizona, where an arrogant young Army major is itching for war. The major's "enemy," the Apache people, had been living in peace for years, but by the time Sundance arrives, the killing has begun again. The soldiers are out for blood, and only Sundance can prevent an all-out war in the desert.

___4561-3 $5.50 US/$6.50 CAN

SUNDANCE

THE MARAUDERS/
DAY OF THE HALFBREEDS
PETER McCURTIN

The Marauders. When Sundance's friend John Tree is gunned down by the notorious Ryker gang, he takes the job of sheriff of Cimmaron City. The last two sheriffs were brutally murdered by the bloodthirsty gang, and now Ryker and his boys aim to take over the town. The terrified townspeople are forced to side with the outlaws, but Sundance would rather face the savage killers alone than turn his back on them.

And in the same action-packed volume . . .

Day of the Halfbreeds. Led by a fanatical madman, the halfbreeds and the fullblooded Indians in Canada are preparing to attack and destroy whites on both sides of the border. A halfbreed himself, Sundance is the logical choice to infiltrate the band of rebels and prevent widespread bloodshed—but will he betray his own people?

___4521-4 $5.50 US/$6.50 CAN